BIND ME TIGHTER STILL

BIND ME TIGHTER STILL

a novel

Lara Ehrlich

Red Hen Press | *Pasadena, CA*

Bind Me Tighter Still
Copyright © 2025 by Lara Ehrlich
All Rights Reserved

No part of this book may be used or reproduced in any manner whatsoever without the prior written permission of both the publisher and the copyright owner. Publisher expressly prohibits the use of this work in connection with the development of any software program, including, without limitation, training a machine learning or generative artificial intelligence (AI) system.

Book design by Mark E. Cull

Library of Congress Cataloging-in-Publication Data

Names: Ehrlich, Lara, 1981– author.
Title: Bind me tighter still: a novel / Lara Ehrlich.
Description: First edition. | Pasadena, CA: Red Hen Press, 2025.
Identifiers: LCCN 2024042074 (print) | LCCN 2024042075 (ebook) | ISBN
  9781636282800 (paperback) | ISBN 9781636282817 (ebook)
Subjects: LCGFT: Fantasy fiction. | Novels.
Classification: LCC PS3605.H7574 B56 2025 (print) | LCC PS3605.H7574
  (ebook) | DDC 813/.6—dc23/eng/20240917
LC record available at https://lccn.loc.gov/2024042074
LC ebook record available at https://lccn.loc.gov/2024042075

Publication of this book has been made possible in part through the financial support of Ann Beman.

The National Endowment for the Arts, the Los Angeles County Arts Commission, the Ahmanson Foundation, the Dwight Stuart Youth Fund, the Max Factor Family Foundation, the Pasadena Tournament of Roses Foundation, the Pasadena Arts & Culture Commission and the City of Pasadena Cultural Affairs Division, the City of Los Angeles Department of Cultural Affairs, the Audrey & Sydney Irmas Charitable Foundation, the Kinder Morgan Foundation, the Meta & George Rosenberg Foundation, the Albert and Elaine Borchard Foundation, the Adams Family Foundation, the Riordan Foundation, Amazon Literary Partnership, and the Mara W. Breech Foundation partially support Red Hen Press.

First Edition
Published by Red Hen Press
www.redhen.org

For Imogen

I love you more than meat loves salt.

BIND ME TIGHTER STILL

We have lingered in the chambers of the sea
By sea-girls wreathed with seaweed red and brown
Till human voices wake us, and we drown.
—"The Love Song of J. Alfred Prufrock," T. S. Eliot

We're not like other women,
We don't have to clean an oven
And we never will grow old,
We've got the world by the tail!
—Theme song of the Weeki Wachee Mermaid Show

PROLOGUE

The siren's hunger is boundless. Ships have advanced on her for centuries aiming their prows at her heart. Their bellies smash against her rock, the Sailor's Ruin, a breaker against a thousand onslaughts. The receding tide reveals an expanse of rotting planks and barnacled bones, but the siren is never satisfied.

A winged figurehead leads a ship in charge along the horizon. The siren calls to her sisters, and they rise from the waves, their nipples peaked in the wind that carries their song like a banner across the sea. The ship turns with a groan and the sailors let the ropes fall slack.

Bound by the sirens' spell, they do not notice that the rock broadens beneath the surface. They do not blink as their ship drives into it, splitting the figurehead's breasts and crushing her wings. The screaming ship casts off its mast and sails. Its hull splinters, and only then do the sailors leap into the sea.

The sirens descend with the ship, gathering scrimshaw portraits, ornate shell boxes, and whalebone corset stays. They drag the sailors down.

One man breaks through the waves with eyes wide and muscles straining, his fair hair curling at his ears. The youngest siren loops her arms around his waist, offering him respite in her embrace. He rests his cheek against her chest, and when his breath has calmed, he looks up into her face, his lips forming around words that die in his mouth.

She knows she is beautiful. She is so fair her veins run beneath her skin like water under ice. Her blue-black hair is thick as rope, her eyes gray as the stormy sea. He loses himself in them. She lowers her mouth to his.

He tastes like sun breaking through the waves. She wraps her tail around his waist, and he moans into her mouth. She slides her lips between his neck and shoulder and opens him just enough to taste him.

He shudders in pain or pleasure; it makes no difference to her. She samples the buttery love he feels for his fiancée, the tang of his regret, the oniony bite of his fear. The brevity of men's lives infuses them with passions unknowable to the siren.

No, her sisters say when she asks if they taste it, too. We just like their meat. But the youngest siren is addicted to their complex taste. The love she has sampled in men surpasses her hunger in intensity, making her feel truly alive for mere moments amidst centuries. She longs to sustain that depth of feeling and claim it as her own.

She slips down the sailor's chest, embracing him as he arches back, his hair dragging in the waves. She tears into his chest to draw out his beating heart between her teeth. When she's had her fill, she lets the sea have what's left of him, basking in the fading glow of his humanity. But still, she is not satisfied.

When the glow is gone, she is empty again. She returns to the sea's arctic cold, her days dark with silt and unchanging. She is driven simply by hunger, no better than a fish, aching until she feeds again.

She wants more than fleeting sensations; she wants to live in them fully, to feel her every cell suffused with love and lust and joy. She wants to understand how human skin and bone can hold so much. She wants to be full.

Her sisters tell her no good can come of longing. They berate her, but punishment only pushes her farther from them. She devours whole ships and returns with the tide, still hungry.

She moves beyond their realm into deeper waters where the waves face her down. The sea is stern and demanding, and she rebels against it, even as she submits to rest cradled in its current, her body wracked with need. She pushes on until she reaches the other edge of the sea. There, she takes a knife to her tail.

1

Sailors from the nearby naval base lean on the bar, as lost on shore as they were at sea. A bartender with one arm that ends in a hook refills their glasses from bottles glinting against a velvet curtain. The sailors barely notice. They are not here for him.

The curtain pulls up to reveal an observation window beyond which arm-length tarpon flash through ice-clear water. A funnel of light glows into existence like the directional beam of a submarine and Ceto emerges into the limestone cavern from a giant plaster conch shell.

Followed by the spotlight, she weaves among a flock of bass impervious to her presence. Her hair billows around her face and tangles in her crown of overlapping shells. A longspine star graces each temple. Clam shells furred with algae clasp her breasts. Her legs are sheathed in a Lycra tail that glitters with silver-tipped scales.

Veiled in bubbles, she arches into a bow-bend, extending her slender arms above her head to welcome four more women into the siren show. Her body follows the course her hands have set, flowing into a backward dive like a curl of smoke. It's so quiet here, as peaceful as if she were in another world.

The sirens run their fingers along the seagrass carpeting the spring floor and glide along the observation windows, serpentine. Their fins flutter like scarves. The bartender winks as Ceto undulates past the window, her razored fluke and sea-storm eyes glittering.

With her tail straight-shot above her, Ceto leads the other sirens in a synchronized plunge to the spring's floor. The terrain of sand and rock is furred with copper-hued weeds that shade to black around the mouth of the spring. The vent, rimmed with jagged teeth of rock, descends into a cave system that burrows through the cliffs.

The sirens clasp hands and shoot up with their arms raised, throwing their heads back, inviting the force of their bodies to lead them into a backward wheel from which they emerge in an arabesque. Jets along the bottom of the windows exhale streams of bubbles up the glass, obscuring the sirens from the audience. They sip from the oxygen hoses concealed among the rocks.

A winged figurehead emerges above the curtain of bubbles leading a plaster ship in charge along the makeshift horizon. The sirens rise from the waves, mouthing the words to the theme song piped into the bar. Ribbons unfurl from their lips.

We are not your average women
We're not yours to bed and keep

The ribbons tangle in the ship's rigging, dragging it into a groaning turn toward a spur of rock.

We want only to be swimmin'

We do not cook; we do not sweep

The ship drives into the rock, splitting the figurehead down her middle.

We are not your average women

We are sirens of the deep

It's Halia's turn to play the sailor tonight. Breaking through the waves, she pantomimes gasping for breath. When Ceto tears the sailor's heart from his chest, some spectators lean in. Some flinch. But no one turns away. She savors their fascinated revulsion.

Although the bar is bleary beyond the window, she can make out two little girls in crowns and mermaid dresses pressing their palms against the glass. She grins at them through the fog of blood she has unleashed. If they do not yet recognize hunger, they will come to know it soon enough. They remind Ceto of own daughter, who is still clinging to the innocence that is fast eluding her.

She's noticed how the sailors have started watching Naia. How their eyes skim the curve of her neck, the dip between her shells, the slope of her stomach. Their objectification of Naia makes her want to rip them apart—and yet, this is the cost of the world she has created for her daughter.

• • •

Deep inside the limestone cliffs, the dressing room is always damp, thundering with the sea that thrashes the cliff face below. It's Naia's favorite place in Sirenland. Cool blue lights wink in the gauze billowing from the ceiling beams. Lounging on their thrones before a row of mirrors framed by shell bulbs, the sirens strip off their tails, revealing their dark-furred legs. They sponge between their thighs and scrub their feet and scrape the salt from their toenails. They wipe down their tails and hang them to dry. Ceto never joins them, allowing her sirens the privacy to meet their needs without scrutiny.

As much as Naia loves this room, it is their space, not hers, a constant reminder that she has no place of her own here. She doesn't even have a mirror. She doesn't need one, her mother says; the audience is her mirror. But at fifteen, Naia has begun to feel the distance between herself and the other sirens, although they have been part of her life for so long they are family. They had lives before Sirenland. Naia knows nothing else.

She leans back on Galene's cot so her aunt can help tug her tail down her thighs, which are pinned together in the ruffled sheath. Galene unpeels the waistband from her hips, shimmying the fabric down her legs until it releases her at last, leaving the imprints of scales on her skin. Her legs are wrinkled and white, and her heels thump to the oriental rug like blocks of wood. Sensation begins to return to them in pinpricks that flare up the backs of her legs.

"Just look at the girl's toes!" Galene says, chafing them between her palms and sending sparks of delicious pain through the soles of Naia's feet. "Her tail's so tight it's cutting off her circulation."

"I know," Nixie snaps at them in the mirror as she strokes her temples with makeup remover. "I'll start a new one after I'm done with your chariot"—she glares at Galene—"and the catfish Mother ordered."

It's a valid excuse, but Naia suspects her aunt likes to see her uncomfortable. Although they are the closest in age, she and Nixie are still divided by a decade and her aunt has always treated her like an annoyance—or worse, a burden.

"She can learn to sew and make it herself," Nixie says as she unhooks her shells—pink with paste jewels she forever loses to the waves. Galene's shells are red and accented with coral filigree. Naia's are white. She knows she's meant to be a blank slate, but she's begun to long for paint and jewels, anything to distance herself from the Aquatic Infant, the outgrown role that sticks to her like a sour smell.

She'd *asked* Nixie to teach her to sew many times, but her aunt said she was too busy until Naia stopped asking. Sewing and designing props for their performances makes her feel useful, Galene explained. It's how she feels she earns her place at Sirenland, just as Maris arranges the music and Halia writes the scripts. Just as Galene raised Naia because her mother possesses many admirable qualities, but tenderness is not one of them.

They've all earned their place here, except Naia who has never had to earn a thing, so Nixie reminds her. It's not her fault; Naia would love to have a special skill to set her apart from the others, but she'd never had the opportunity to learn what she's good at, other than performing.

"Come now," Halia says, pulling her comb through Maris's long hair. "Remember when *you* were her age? Give her a little grace."

Nixie narrows her eyes at them in the mirror and drops her shells into her lap, taunting Halia with her full breasts.

When she'd arrived at Sirenland, Halia had hidden her patchy scalp with wigs, abandoning them only when her hair had grown past her shoulders. She hasn't so much as trimmed it since. When Naia threatens to cut her own tangled hair, her aunt winds it around her wrists and says, "You never miss such things until they're gone."

Although she jokes about her hair, Halia has never spoken of the scars on the plane of her chest, which she'd hidden with tattooed shells long before she'd pilgrimaged to Sirenland.

Maris plucks jewels from her cheeks and wipes glitter from her own tattooed shells, identical to Halia's. With their lean torsos and flowing hair, dyed matching green, they could be twins. They test new looks on each other, side by side in their mirrors, and sleep in each other's arms.

Even as a child, Naia had known that her aunts were formed in the crucible of a world beyond her understanding. Halia had set out to help people and ended up in corporate law. Maris had spent her boyhood constructing forts in fathomless woods. Nixie had made supper every night for herself and a younger brother she no longer speaks to. Even Galene, Ceto's first siren, still sometimes betrays the influence of her former life; she'd honed her ability to anticipate their needs through decades in customer service and a marriage she never talks about.

Naia knows nothing more about herself than that she was born in Sirenland. All her mother will tell her is that one night, just that once, she'd slipped into the bar beyond the glass in a borrowed dress. The sailors had crashed at her knees, she says. One had stolen her away—and stolen her will.

What color was the dress? Naia asks. How did the room smell? What did the music sound like, without water in your ears? Do I look like my father? Her mother only ever says one thing: Your father is of no consequence.

Naia seeks commonality with her mother, but although Ceto presses her close at night, she remains as distant as the horizon. So, she has adopted her aunts' stories as her own; she'll catch herself wondering why she didn't inherit Maris's quick wit or Nixie's artistry, Halia's enthusiasm for solving complex problems or Galene's patience, and she'll remember, startled anew each time, that she is bound to them by nothing more than shared experience.

She has no history of her own, no personality other than the Aquatic Infant, who she no longer wants to be, and hadn't chosen in the first place. She doesn't think she is like her mother, and Ceto refuses to say if she is like her father. So, who is she then?

The question had always nagged at her, but the older she gets and the tighter her tail, the more insistent it becomes.

Galene opens their door to the knock of the one-armed bartender, the only staff allowed into Sirenland's inner sanctum. He passes her a dinner cart and retreats into the industrial hallway. Galene closes the door, securing them inside their dressing room.

The sirens crowd around the cart, loading their plates with glistening sashimi and piles of seaweed and prawns as big as their fists.

"Come eat," Galene beckons to Naia. "You're getting too thin."

"I'm not hungry," she lies. She is ravenous, but so tired of fish sliding down her throat and seaweed catching in her teeth, the silty bitterness of clam bellies and the mineral sweetness of crabs. Her aunts have told her about dishes with exotic flavors and textures; dishes they eat in their dreams and recount to one another with longing they don't otherwise indulge in.

"Tell me again about pizza?" Naia prompts them.

Halia throws her head back with a loud, joyful snort. Maris joins in with her own basso laugh. Galene straps on her leather shells and flips her tasseled whip across her shoulder. She's late for her private show.

Once, when Naia was young, she had risked her mother's wrath to find out what they meant by the "private show." She'd lingered behind her aunts in the tank, determined to discover what happens beyond the bed of seagrass in the corner. She'd pushed through it to find the entrance to an offshoot cave just large enough for one siren. A single pane of glass set into the back of the cave had reflected Naia's wide eyes back to her. She still doesn't know what happens there.

"Shall I send up some scallops?" Galene asks.

"It's not about the *food*," Naia moans, flopping back on Galene's bed.

"What is it, honey?" Maris asks.

Halia slides into her twin's lap with a reassuring smile at Naia.

"I just want..." she trails off, struggling to articulate her desires. "I just want to try something *else*. Something different than this—but I don't know what. I don't know what else there even is."

"I've tried everything at least twice, and nothing comes close to what we have here," Halia says. "Pizza aside."

"Stop talking about food." Nixie stretches out naked on her cot and folds her hands across her stomach as it whines with hunger. Her punishment ended yesterday, but Nixie has continued fasting as testament to her devotion. "If you don't want to be here, then go. Leave sirenhood to those who've earned it."

"Don't pay her any mind. That's just hunger talking." Galene shakes out Naia's second-best tail and stretches open the tightest part at the fluke.

"I'm not hungry," Nixie mutters, as her stomach complains again. She closes her eyes and curls toward the wall. Without her ribbons and jewels, she looks like any other woman. Her blonde hair turns ragged at her waist.

Naia forces her feet into her fluke and represses a groan as her aunt helps tug the fabric up her thighs, sealing her up again. Naia has never understood why she is the only siren who must wear a tail at all times; the only one who enjoys no respite from her mother's surveillance.

She takes this thought with her to the oyster shell, where she lies awake, her tail entwined with her mother's. The shell rests on a raised dais in the center of the room, surrounded by seawater funneled in from the ocean that laps at the shell's ridges. The waves sigh below the window that frames the sea where Naia was born, and Ceto was born again, her mother says.

The oyster's silk lining is slippery and cool, but Naia is folded into her mother's moist heat. As a child, she had sought comfort in this ritual, the only time Ceto had shown her any affection. Naia had looked forward to these stifling nights, longing for warmth from her mother who was otherwise as cold as the sea.

Naia still hungers for this closeness, but lately she's begun to notice how she must bend to fit her mother's contours, how her thighs are smashed together in her tail. Her legs ache to stretch out, itch to feel the sheets against the undersides of her knees. She longs to take up space.

Her mother clutches her to her chest as if she were still a child. She kisses her neck just below the ear. Sometimes, Naia feels her mother's teeth graze her jugular, feels her blood slip down her skin. Ceto never takes much.

2

Strongwomen from the nearby boardwalk carry the sirens' thrones through Sirenland's inner sanctum. Pipes gurgle above them. Their jeweled hair glints under the fluorescent lights lining the ceiling of the tunnel. Ceto forbids her sirens to leave the dressing room without their tails or to navigate land with anything less than regal grace.

"—and I told that bitch, come at me again and you'll find out," Nixie regales her sisters. She had taken to sirenhood more quickly than the others, a natural in a tail and in the tank, but no amount of practice could smooth away her rough-hewn edges. To Ceto, she's a cautionary tale for what happens to a daughter when failed by her mother.

As the sirens pass through a padlocked door into the sunlight they fall silent and adopt the exaggerated expressions of their personas. Ceto need no longer check behind her to ensure that Nixie adopts her candy-pink pout, or Naia the innocent mask she's worn since childhood. The door closes behind them to be hidden again behind a screen of maiden grass. They emerge onto the beach.

Throughout the centuries, the waves have carved a crescent into the cliffs, forming a cove sheltered from the violence of the sea. A fishing boat glides on the horizon. Gulls launch from the rock the sirens call the Sailor's Ruin, a hundred yards from shore. A foghorn sounds.

The strongwomen position the sirens' thrones atop six coral daises arranged along the ocean's edge and retreat into the cliffs. Photographers, one assigned to each siren, wait at the ready as guests begin to descend the driftwood path zigzagging down the cliff from the parking lot. They are accompanied by the tinny music of the Ferris wheel at the end of the boardwalk. Naia had taken her first independent steps on this beach, reaching out to the wheel that spins deep into the night, tracing dizzy lights across the sea.

The repetitive tune grates on Ceto's nerves. She misses the silence that had greeted her when she'd first arrived at what had been a godforsaken spot along the highway. There had been nothing for miles, except a wind-bent tree grasping at the air, a canted picnic table, and a clapboard building. On the sign above the door, a mermaid whose shells barely concealed her breasts had grimaced into the distance. Cursive script along her tail read, "Sirenland, est. 1945." This place had been nothing before Ceto. She had turned a defunct roadside attraction into a kingdom.

A new world had emerged around Sirenland, inspired by Ceto's vision, and grown beyond her grasp. The boardwalk had unspooled along the beach, jagging into the pier that now extends into the sea. The Ferris wheel had risen first, followed by hot dog stands, ice cream parlors, and clam shacks. Motels had sprung up like mushrooms along the strip of highway bordering the beach. Tourist shops began to peddle taffy, painted shells, hemp necklaces, soap, fudge.

Performers had courted Ceto for her blessing to set up on the boardwalk, and she'd granted it for a cut of their profits, maintaining an illusion of authority. She'd blessed a strongwoman and a pin man, a witch with a two-headed cat, an artist who paints his sitters' souls. She promoted the mythos that evolved around Sirenland and encouraged its commodification: all the shops along the boardwalk must carry the sirens' likenesses on postcards, T-shirts, keychains, mugs, and magnets, and every drinking establishment must offer the rum cocktail, Sailor's Ruin. And yet, Ceto holds Sirenland apart. Her sirens are forbidden to leave its grounds or consort with performers from the boardwalk.

"This is not a freak show," she tells them. "We must not be associated with fortune tellers and bearded ladies."

It's an uneasy balance. To perpetuate the myth, she's had to cheapen it. But without this world she's created, she'd be nothing again.

As the guests roil onto her beach, Ceto resigns herself to the seemingly endless procession of little girls in mermaid dresses eager to run their dirty hands over her scales. They are just barely held in check by signs posted along the path that read "Don't touch the sirens," accompanied by jars of fingers. She scans the teen girls with their grassy sweat stink, the balding men whose guts would pop between her teeth, the young brides whose blood would be sweet with hope and spiced with uncertainty.

Her annual suitor pushes past small children to reach her first. He has come every summer for the better part of a decade, his face swelling, his stomach inflating with every passing year.

"Spare a second for me?" Nixie beckons him with a throaty growl as he stalks past her throne. She arches her back, shaking her long blond hair over her shoulders, and blows him a kiss, but he doesn't acknowledge her. "Oh, daddy, don't ignore me."

Halia and Maris flip their tails at him from their conjoined throne.

"Hey, sailor," they call to him. "Spend a few minutes with us?"

Galene cracks her whip in his path. Naia shrinks down in her throne as he passes, but he doesn't even glance in her direction, and stops only at the end of the line before Ceto, devouring her with his eyes.

As her suitor pushes a bundle of roses into her arms, Ceto appraises his meaty palms. Her teeth would melt easily through the thick layer of fat to the bone.

The photographer settles a crown on the man's balding head and hands him a plastic trident. As her suitor takes his place on the top step of the dais, gazing up at her in adoration, Ceto sucks in her belly and pushes her breasts toward him. She flashes the sly grin she'd perfected, envisioning the row of photos along his bedroom wall, her beauty fading in the progression of summers. As always, he buys the complete photo package, including the keychain.

A girl little older than Naia takes his place with a shy head bob. Her sunburnt shoulders curve self-consciously, and her hip bones stick out above the frayed waistband of her shorts. Ceto disdains her, and all the little girls who spill onto the pavement shimmering with heat, their damp hair adhered to their cheeks. These pimpled, myopic girls come to Sirenland to convince themselves that magic exists; that proximity to sirens will imbue them with power they don't inherently possess. They leave Sirenland with plastic shells and polyester tails that rip on the way home.

Naia loves the smallest guests, with their funny questions and their belief in the ability to pass from the real world into one of magic as easily as crossing the parking lot. She sneaks a glance at her mother in the throne beside her, and finding her preoccupied, lifts a little girl onto her lap.

Her mother's attention to such minor transgressions has waned as Naia has grown out of her childish compulsion to push boundaries. She no longer refuses to wear her tail or tries to sneak into minivans or asks other people's mothers to take her to the Ferris wheel.

She has cultivated more subtle ways to gather information

about the forbidden world beyond Sirenland. She eavesdrops on guests' conversations, willing them to expand on mysterious subjects like school and friends and bicycles. While to the young girls waiting in line, the sirens are enchanting, to Naia it's the guests whose lives are edged with magic. Theirs is a world foreign to her, and becoming ever more alluring as her awareness of it sharpens.

What began as a fascination with other children has become a steady craving for the sensations denied to her: the feel of sand between her toes, tastes and textures other than raw fish, hearing her own voice ring out across the beach. With these simple imagined pleasures dominating her daydreams, she cannot begin to express the more intense desires beginning to roil beneath them.

The child on her lap is greasy with sunscreen and slips on her scales. Naia steadies her with one hand as the child's eyes trace her cheekbones, her eyelids and lips. The little girl's mother calls to her, coaxing her to look at the camera, but she's enthralled, stroking Naia's tail, her eyes soft and wondering. The tail is designed for a child, after all.

Naia savors the featherlike sensation of her little fingers, their tentative and wondering exploration so different from her mother's ironlike grip or her aunts' efficient grooming. Sensing Ceto's eyes on her, Naia straightens for the picture. It's such a small thing, this innocent touch, and worth every ounce of her mother's disapproval.

The flashbulb goes off and the little girl's mother lifts her from

Naia's lap. The loss of the girl's warm weight leaves Naia strangely bereft.

Two boys and a girl take the child's place before the throne. Although the boys stare at a fixed point over Naia's head, their red cheeks betray their interest. Naia is more concerned with the way the girl's legs emerge from the petals of her ruffled pink beach dress. The dip between her collarbones is damp and her ponytail is fraying from its rubber band. She lifts one bare foot and scratches behind the opposite knee with dirty toes. She smells like bug spray.

The girl studies Naia's tail with her hands buried in the pockets of her dress.

When she was seven, Naia snuck a little girl into the dressing room. They played dress-up in her aunts' costumes and jewels and swore to be best friends forever. When the girl's parents had finally noticed she was gone, panic had erupted throughout Sirenland. The Coast Guard had shut down the beach and the police locked down the bar—until Galene had found Naia and the girl sleeping in the oyster shell wrapped in each other's arms.

Ceto had returned the child to her family with apologies and gift cards to the boardwalk and reassurances that of course bad things do not happen here; never *here* at Sirenland. When they'd finally gone, she'd sliced off Naia's little toe.

The photographer waves over the girl in the confectionery dress and Naia grins at her as if to say: *Won't you be my friend and tell me everything about bicycles?* The girl scowls in return, thrusting her hands deeper into her lace-lined pockets. Naia flinches as she had when her mother's knife had nicked through her bone. She fails at mastering even the fundamentals of friendship.

The girl flops onto her stomach at the foot of Naia's throne and the photographer fits a plastic tail over her legs. She looks up at the two boys flanking the throne, but they don't acknowledge her. They're too busy pretending not to look at Naia. The one to her right—who shares the girl's stout frame and surly expression—leans close to Naia. His breath tickles the inside of her ear, carrying with it the same fried meat smell that wafts to Sirenland from the boardwalk.

"He thinks you're pretty," he stage-whispers to her, lifting his eyebrows toward his friend. A flush dapples the other boy's pale skin, darkening his freckles. His features are too big for his lean scaffolding. His damp hair flops over his forehead.

Naia is used to being told she's pretty. Mothers and little girls and old men have told her she's pretty all her life, but this hoarse whisper is different and makes her feel exposed. She wraps her arms across her bare stomach.

"She smells like fish," the girl says with a sharp laugh.

Resisting the urge to bite a chunk out of the girl's plump cheek, she sticks out her tongue when the camera flashes.

"Can he get your number?" the surly boy asks, shooting a glance at his friend, who closes his eyes as if willing himself to disappear.

"I fear I do not understand your request," Naia says, tipping her head in mock confusion, obeying the rules of Sirenland: *Cast your eyes at the water. Carry your voice like the whisper of waves. Wear your hair long and unbound. Do not betray knowledge of the world beyond Sirenland, and direct any questions you cannot answer to the information kiosk.*

"I told you they have to stay in character," the girl says, as the photographer removes the plastic tail. "So lame."

"Sorry about that," the freckled boy mumbles to Naia. He turns away, only to be jerked back to the throne by Naia's hair that's become tangled in his shirt buttons. Blushing, he works to unsnarl it with fumbling fingers, his head lowered before her.

The exposed skin at the back of his neck is flushed from the sun. She wants to press her lips there and taste its heat. The sudden temptation steals her breath, leaving her dizzy as if she were trapped beneath the waves. She brushes his fingers aside to free herself, wishing she could chop off her hair. She wonders what her mother would do to her.

The girl grabs his hand, glaring at Naia. As she begins to tug him playfully toward the ocean, Naia flips her fluke in front of the girl's feet, and she drops to her knees. The boy, startled, laughs. When the girl glances up at him, her angry eyes blurred with tears, he reaches down to help her. She swats his hand away and scrambles to her feet.

"You did that on purpose," she snarls at Naia.

"I fear I do not understand," Naia says, her voice like the whisper of waves.

The girl starts up the dais toward Naia, her hands screwed in fists.

"Stop!" Ceto's voice cracks down the line, then softens as she addresses the girl. "Come here, child."

The girl backs off the dais and approaches Ceto with glazed wonder. Naia well knows that transfixion. It's why she had calmly placed her foot on the cutting board and yielded to all other punishments without complaint, folding herself into a lobster cage, holding herself beneath the sea to the drowning point.

Her mother grasps the girl's wrist and pulls her close, whispering into her flushed face. The girl nods, docile, unblinking, until Ceto releases her with a gentle push that sends her stumbling across the beach. Naia might feel sorry for a girl who is so easily subjugated, but saves her sympathy for herself.

The guests invade the sea with flailing limbs and paddle boards, their tsunami thighs thrashing beneath them. Naia pities them for their dependence on oxygen and their vulgar pleasure in the world that, to her, is home. She drifts beneath them, pinching their toes and laughing at their shrieking retreat toward shore. She knows it's childish, but it's such a harmless amusement and she has so few pleasures.

Her aunts take Siren Swim more seriously than she does. For three hours a day, it's the sirens' duty to grant their guests the pleasure of swimming among them in their sacred cove. Some flounder around in cheap tails from the gift shop, some sketch the sirens in their natural habitat, others believe this cove possesses healing properties. The gift shop also sells vials of seawater supposedly collected by the sirens at midnight. That was Naia's idea.

She laughs watching Nixie lead dilettantes in tails through her most complicated tricks, putting their amateur efforts to shame. Halia and Maris intertwine in the surf, stroking one another's hair with shell-encrusted combs. Galene teaches a flock of little girls how to swan dive under Ceto's watchful gaze. She observes them all from the Sailor's Ruin where she lounges with an eel sliding around her waist.

Girls bake on towels along the thin strip of sand. Naia admires their glistening legs as her own shins itch and her ankle bones grind together in her tail. She usually longs to lie among the girls, sunning herself in the radiance of their affection. Today she wants to tear them apart.

The girl who had mocked her stands at the water's edge, tempting the waves that scrabble toward her, riding one another's backs to the beach. She scuttles away at the last second, out of reach of the ocean's grasp. It chases her across the beach, back to the boys who wrestle in the sand, watching Naia.

The girl cocks her hips and lifts her chin to lengthen her neck, reminding Naia of a preening seagull. She tosses her dress onto her towel, casting a glance at the freckled boy. He is still staring at Naia—but she is watching the girl as she tugs at the hem of her bikini, stretching the fabric's polka-dots into ovals. The boys streak past her and launch into the sea. She wades after them, leaving her belongings on the beach.

"Watch it," someone shouts, buffeting Naia with an inner tube.

She dips below the surface again, into the silent pantomime of legs. Beneath her extends a pasture of vivid green weeds that glow as the sun slants through the surface and deepen into shades of rust under the cover of clouds. Panfish flash like coins circling the algae-cloaked base of the Sailor's Ruin, and startlingly blue damselfish pass in and out of a carpet anemone's brain-like ripples.

Naia traces the landscape she knows by heart to the limestone wall that shields the cove from the wind. There, she'd long ago found a vent, an entrance into the cave system that burrows through Sirenland. She knows better than to explore its labyrinthian depths; she'd heard stories of divers who had lost their way following the current through the branching chambers as if through a giant heart.

Naia stores her treasures below an overhanging shelf just inside the vent. There, she has a collection of silverware from picnic baskets, half a dozen watches, an assortment of jewelry, and books she'd stolen from beachgoers' bags, along with other artifacts out of which she's constructed a piecemeal understanding of the world beyond the beach. The tide or an enterprising octopus gifts her sea glass, shells, bits of bone. She keeps her spoils in a waterproof sack she'd appropriated from a local fishmonger. While she can rarely escape her mother's watchful gaze long enough to enjoy her treasures, just knowing they're here gives her a sense of connection to the outside world and feeds her increasing need to push back against Ceto's stifling rule.

Hugging the limestone wall, Naia rides the waves ashore with the sack slung over her shoulder. Guests leave their towels and umbrellas and picnic baskets scattered along the beach as they scavenge shells from Naia's cove. It's only fair that she robs them in return.

The sunbathers flip onto their stomachs, alone on the beach; the other guests are marinating in the sea. Naia drags the girl's towel across the sand, her purse and discarded dress along with it. The scent of bug spray wafts from her belongings. The girl is still paddling after the boys, who are competing to catch the biggest wave, as Naia stuffs the bundle into her sack. She slips back into the sea to stow her plunder under the rock shelf, hurrying now so Ceto won't notice her absence. The last time a siren failed to show up on time—Maris has made no secret of her hatred for Siren Swim—she'd gone without food until she was too weak to beg for it.

Naia joins a school of redfish riding the current toward shore. In the foaming surf, she spots the girl thrashing her legs, expending unnecessary energy in pursuit of the boys. Naia skims the seagrass to glide below the girl's pale belly. The guests are so vulnerable in the sea, so easily scared when they can't see what's beneath them. Naia delights in harmless torments, and this girl deserves to be put in her place. She scrabbles at the swath of bare skin above her, and the girl jerks and thrashes, and like a squid releases a blinding cloud of urine.

Naia plunges twenty yards away to rise choking on laughter near the Sailor's Ruin. Her mother glances down at her in warning, and she wipes her face clear of expression.

She clasps the rock, watching the freckled boy splash his friend. He glances at Naia and away, as if she burns his eyes. Lean bands of muscle along his stomach shift with his breath. Naia catches his skittish gaze and startles at the sudden tug between them, as physical as if he'd jerked on a rope tethered to her belly. His eyes widen. Had he felt it too? The boy throws his shoulders back in mock confidence and plunges into the waves.

As he thrashes toward her, his breaststroke clumsy and unpracticed, the bond tightens below her rib cage. Naia backs further out, testing the distance between them. The connection unspools in her gut, a strange sensation as if her intestines were unwinding, as if she were towing him along with her. He pauses beyond the Sailor's Ruin, treading water, panting. Naia flows toward and then beneath him, skimming her fingers along the soles of his feet. She coils around him, allowing his palms to graze her shoulders, and rises against him, chest to chest. Something hard juts against the seam of her tail. She leans into him, squinting into his eyes.

"Hi," he says, breathless. Sunburnt skin peels from the ridges of his brows.

She smiles, bewildered by the tingle that darts down her stomach at his touch, the deep ache it awakens inside her.

"Hi," she says, wondering what's next.

He parts his lips, but he seems to have run out of breath, far too soon. She often forgets that her stamina is unrivaled even among the sirens. And yet, she is disappointed in this boy, although she couldn't begin to explain, even to herself, what she'd expected of him. As she backs away, he paddles after her. His nose dips below the surface. He rises with a gasp and dips again, his eyes clinging to hers. The heat of his gaze is thrilling and unexpected, and shoots an answering spark down her body. She draws him back, fanning the spark.

At the net barrier marking Sirenland's edge, the boy strains to raise his chin. He labors to breathe, but Naia holds him fast with nothing more than her gaze. He opens his mouth and the sea pours in. His eyes plead with her. The power she wields over him is exhilarating, so pleasurable it's painful. She closes the distance between them and presses her lips to his. Their wet mouths slide against each other. She wants to succumb to the sensation, to drown in it. But she forces her eyes open, sustaining her link with this boy who tastes like salt and something sweet she doesn't recognize. Determined to find out what it is, she grinds her lips harder against his, her teeth against his teeth.

She tastes blood, along with a rush of salt and intense fear, his insecurity and something else breaking through the crust of his innocence, a longing for something primal and heady that she can't put a name to, but that she has felt within herself deeply, shamefully, when folded into her mother's body, wishing the heat her skin radiated belonged to someone else. She is engulfed in the sensation of recognition, of shared longing for experience beyond her understanding.

As the boy goes under, his fingers tangle in her hair, dragging her down with him. The ripping pain against her skull snaps her out of her daze. She pulls him up against the current, but he is a dead weight, his eyes riveted to hers. She grips him against her chest, pushing for shore.

At last, the sea takes pity on her. The waves scoop her up, and she rests cradled in their gentle thrusts until her tail scrapes the sand. She hauls the boy onto the beach, conscious of the intimacy of her arms around his chest, and rolls him to his back. Naia pushes herself up beside him. There is sand in his eyelashes. His chest stutters, and then to her relief begins to rise and fall. He opens his eyes to Ceto's daughter.

• • •

Naia has broken Sirenland's essential law and consorted with a guest. She should be banished immediately—if she were any other siren, she would be—but Ceto knows the hunger that led her to lead that boy onward just to see how deep she could go. She'd built Sirenland so Naia would never know such hunger. But it's part of her, Ceto now understands, and can no more be ignored than an approaching storm. She'd been foolish to think otherwise.

Perhaps she should not have kept Naia innocent of the world beyond Sirenland. To an ignorant woman, a man becomes teacher in all things. Ceto well remembers her education.

She slides off the Sailor's Ruin into the calming sea as the past rises up to meet her.

Long ago, in another life, she had washed ashore with her legs tangled in the tatters of her tail. Unprepared for the full force of the earth towing her down, she'd pulled herself upright bone by bone, trembling with the effort. The sensation of knives plunging into her heels nearly brought her to her knees again, but she would not bow to pain. She stood firm as the sea wrenched at her feet, trying to reclaim her.

The sun rose behind her, casting her shadow on the sand. The beach was deserted, the silence thinner than the sea's thick hush. Dunes rose out of scrubby grass at the edge of the beach. She choked as air fills her lungs in a great gust, used as she was to gills' measured breath.

A creature darted yowling over the dunes. She refused to cower as it leapt at her, clawing at her bare thighs, awakening her to the frailty of her humanity. She'd smashed sharks with her fluke and torn apart bigger men than herself with her teeth, but this human body was not built for savagery. She didn't even know how to use her legs.

A voice snapped across the beach, and a man appeared atop the dunes. His chest was bare. He wore a towel over his shoulder and carried his shoes in one hand. He ran toward her, shouting at the animal. He grasped a band around its neck and yanked the animal down to the sand. It peeled back its lips at her.

His voice gentle now, the man reached out to her, uttering sounds she didn't understand. She shook her head. His cheeks reddened as he took in her nakedness, and his concern deepened into confused hunger.

He spoke again, venturing to wrap his towel around her, and she shook her head. No, I don't understand, and looked into his eyes, appealing to men's cursed need to protect. She had used their need against them for hundreds of years. She took his hand in her salt-roughened palm. What made him different from the other men she had destroyed? Nothing but her humanity.

She was curious about love, so she went with the man to his home far from the ocean where he'd been merely a visitor. He drove faster than she could swim, over land that shifted from gold to green made vibrant by the relentless sun. Her stomach was sour and she rested her forehead against the window as the rolling ground leveled out and the grass turned coarse and brown. They came to a place where the land was flatter than the sky. Crows eyed her from the gabled roof of the farmhouse. The man slipped a ring on her finger and carried her over his threshold.

"Welcome home, darlin'," he whispered against her cheek. Just inside the door, he pressed his tongue to the hinge of her jaw and traced lingering kisses along her bared neck until he met her lips. She had never been kissed; never even been touched. It sent sparks into her belly.

She reveled in the discovery of herself and her humanity. She wore tapered slacks that accentuated her calves and swept her waist-length hair into a sleek French twist, and was still the most exotic person for hundreds of miles. She used her talent for convincing people to want what they didn't need to convince the town factory to want her as an office manager. She worked hard. She learned to cook and clean and to speak in her husband's tongue. When he asked how she came to be on the beach, she said she couldn't remember; her life began that day.

She went to church, where she sat beside her husband in his ancestral pew, wearing a hat with no purpose as the pastor strove to bind the congregation to a higher power.

"The mouth of the righteous is a well of life," he said. "But violence covers the mouth of the wicked."

She had no patience for good or evil, or her husband's rituals. But she played along, committed to discovering what it meant to be human—to be what they called a "good wife."

The days passed like relentless waves that rocked her back each time she found her footing. She experienced desire and boredom, fleeting joy and, ever more often, doubt—but none of the richer sensations for which she'd shorn her tail. Soon, one emotion transcended all others: loneliness.

Even in its immensity, the sea connects all life; as a siren, she could hear her sisters calling, whales singing, the fluttering tentacles of a jellyfish. The waves had carried her voice in ever-widening rings that reverberated off distant shores and returned to her months later. She could always orient herself. Now, her thoughts were trapped inside her own head and offered poor company. Her husband said he loved her, that he couldn't live without her, but that didn't make her feel any less alone.

Soon, she'd cleaned every inch of the farmhouse and explored every inch of her husband's body. She knew what brought him pleasure, but he never found what brought her pleasure in return. His lust for her settled into a deep, calm love. The days passed like ripples lapping at the edge of a lake. She didn't want a deep, calm love. She wanted a tsunami.

She could no longer bear for him to press alongside her in bed, to rest his weight on her, sling his arm across her belly. Everything in this world was too heavy, oppressed by its own mass. Humans moved and spoke too fast, and touched too hard.

"Don't touch me!" she wanted to scream. But that wouldn't be fair to her husband, who wanted only to please her, to run his palms along her thighs. She bit off screams, resenting him for being blind to her anguish, even as she hid it from him.

"Do you ever want to try new dishes?" she asked her neighbor Linda as they carried platters of steak and potatoes to their husbands at Linda's dining room table.

Linda had grown up in this house, where she now lived with her own family as if her life had slid into that of her parents' and carried on. It seemed like such a meager existence, untethered to any significance beyond that prescribed by a made-up god.

"Jim likes beef," Linda said and turned away.

Ceto's stomach cramped. She was always starving. She took her seat, allowing the husbands' conversation to wash over her as she abandoned dinner in favor of red wine. She refilled her glass again and again, drinking to quell her hunger.

"I'm lonely," she told her husband as they crossed the field back to their house—*his* house, where he'd grown up.

"We have each other, darlin'," he said.

He brought her flowers and talked about his day. He explained the properties of thermodynamics, although she couldn't follow and didn't care. He built a cradle.

As she stood at the window with her palms pressed to the cliff edge of her belly, her loneliness began to recede. She was connected to another body, waiting curled inside her. The ocean of her womb carried the child's heartbeats in ever-widening circles. She could feel its emotions, its simple contentment, like barnacles riding on the backs of whales, grateful for the refuge.

During endless meetings and evenings at home, she turned her attention inward, communing with her child. The connection tethered her. She was content within the world of herself. It did not last long.

3

The sirens prepare for the evening show in silence, averting their eyes from Naia. Their faces shimmer in their mirrors like tropical fish. Galene skims blush along the swell of her cheeks to create the suggestion of angles. She prefers bold colors: the red of blood fresh from the vein, the purple of lightning-lit clouds. Nixie presses a swath of fishnet to her skin and streaks silver and green paint from her cheekbones to her temples. She strips the netting away to reveal a pattern of scales.

"So, how was it?" Nixie breaks the silence, catching Naia's eyes in the mirror. She pouts, layering hues of glitter-infused lipstick to achieve a metallic sheen.

"What?" Naia's breath catches and she bows her head over her tail, scraping mildew from the dorsal fin with her fingernail.

"What?" Nixie mimics her, widening her eyes in a parody of innocence as she fits featherlike fins over her ears. They are her own creation, as is the scaled collar dripping with pearls that plunges between her breasts.

"We saw you kiss that boy. Since the rest of us have sworn off men, the least you can do is tell us how it was." She swivels from her mirror, fixing her attention on Naia with unnerving intensity.

Naia blushes, recalling his dark eyelashes and the quick rise and fall of his chest, the power she'd held over him and her fleeting willingness to let him drown. It's possible she's exaggerating—how bold to imagine she wields power over life and death! But there was the way he'd gazed at her, as if lost in her eyes. Even as his friends had supported him across the beach, he had stared back at her with dumb longing, as transfixed by her as she was by the taste of his blood. Its nauseating sweetness lingers on her tongue.

Ceto has tasted all of her sirens. Naia knows by the matching crescents along their jugulars, and yet they've never spoken of it. Her mother's hunger has always just been part of life in Sirenland, as natural as their dance, as necessary as their punishments. Naia had never questioned it. But when the boy's blood passed her lips, she'd awoken to a strange new kinship with Ceto. As much as she'd always longed for a connection with her mother, this was not what she'd envisioned. She'd always felt oppressed by Ceto's need for control, and it was horrifying to realize she might have inherited her mother's hunger for dominating others. The depth and viciousness of that hunger left her breathless.

Let them think it was just a kiss.

"How angry do you think Mother will be?" she asks Galene, who has been Ceto's companion for as long as she can remember.

But her aunt busies herself arranging Naia's shells and comb on the bed. The twins exchange a look heavy with concern as Maris traces the shells on Halia's chest with makeup glue and dusts the pattern with glitter.

"Very," Nixie says. "If any of *us* had done what you did, she would feed us to the sharks."

None of Naia's aunts are strangers to punishment, and for far less grievous transgressions. Nixie is still atoning for yawning in the photo line. She hasn't eaten in three days.

"Don't worry, she'll go easier on you." Bitterness creeps into Nixie's voice. "Now, tell us how it was."

Naia's breath quickens with the memory of the boy's blood, and her power.

"Confusing."

Halia laughs as she presses gems along the ridges of Maris's ribs.

"I remember my first," Halia says. "In second grade I brought cupcakes to school for my birthday and dropped them on the rug. Doug Riggs helped me pick lint off the icing and convinced everyone they were still good. I loved him from that moment—for years!—but I was too shy to talk to him. On a high school band trip we ended up sitting next to each other on the bus. It was a long ride and I was so thrilled to be next to him that I just stared out the window, barely breathing, for hours."

Halia's hands flutter to her lap and come to rest. She closes her eyes.

"The other kids watched movies and listened to music and talked across the aisle. Finally, the bus got dark and quiet. As I was falling asleep, I felt Doug's hand on my knee. I looked at him, wondering if he meant for his hand to be there, and he swooped in with a kiss. He was shaking so much our braces scraped. When I kissed him back, he put his arms around me. We kissed for a long time in that dark, quiet bus—and then we never kissed, or even spoke, again."

Halia smiles a little, and Naia can't quite place the emotion behind it. Conversations with her aunts always spiral out of her grasp.

"I still think about Doug, and that bus ride, a lot, actually."

"Very romantic," Nixie says, rolling her eyes. "Mine was with my stepdad, and that wasn't all he did when he snuck into my room. What about you, Maris? Was your first kiss with a nice girl who smelled like flowers?"

"That's enough," Maris says in her stern, gentle voice, and to her twin: "I can see why you'd hold onto that memory, and I'm glad you have it. I'm sorry others of us have had experiences we'd prefer to forget."

She leans over and squeezes Nixie's balled fist. "No," she says, "it was not with a girl who smelled like flowers."

Nixie glares into the mirror as if Maris doesn't exist. But her fist relaxes under Maris's palm. She slides her fingers free and picks up her brush again.

The sirens lapse into silence, leaning close to their mirrors to apply the final strokes that complete their transformations. Galene hitches up Naia's tail until it bites into her belly and pulls her into a quick hug.

"It'll be okay," she says. "If your mother seems harsh, it's only because she's protecting you—protecting us all."

From *what*, Naia wants to ask, but she knows they won't answer.

Naia shifts on the damp floor of the bunker, a tiled room constructed around the tube that descends twenty feet through concrete and cliff and into the tank, the sirens' entrance to another world.

Naia squeezes with her aunts around the opening of the tube and the sirens join hands. As they bow their heads in prayer to the Great Mother, the sea, Naia steals a glance at her aunts, hoping to catch someone's eye. They are unwavering in their devotion. She is alone in her disquiet.

"The mouth of the righteous is a well of life," Ceto says. She is austere in contrast to the other sirens' finery. Her tail is black with silver-tipped scales. Her shells, too, are black and crusted with barnacles. Her face is clear. Makeup would be redundant; her cheeks are always high red against her pale skin, her eyes sphinxlike beneath her lashes. Her only ornamentation is her crown.

"The mouth of the righteous is a well of life," the sirens repeat and slip one by one into the tube. Naia slides off the rim after Nixie, tensing as the ocean's chill surges up her belly. She grips the metal ladder bolted along the tube's interior and pulls herself down into the darkness, against the pressure of the sea.

Although Naia has made this journey since she was a child, the frigid plunge through the darkness has lost none of its mystery. She focuses on delving into the heart of the cliff she calls home, startled as always by the transition between worlds when she emerges from the end of the tube hidden within the giant plaster conch shell. She swims out into the tank, appearing to the audience as if by magic. She's always loved her role in creating the illusion that enchants the people beyond the glass, but she's begun to wonder why she must maintain the illusion in private. Why must she wear a tail at all times, even to bed, where there is no audience to beguile?

Ceto descends last, into the crown of the sirens' upraised arms, and they fall in line before the windows, swaying their hips and mouthing the lyrics of the Siren's Song refrain: *We are not your average women / We are sirens of the deep.*

A curtain of bubbles sails up the windows and Naia takes her place on the plaster rock. As the effervescence fades, Galene rides across the windows in a chariot. She bears a whip over one shoulder, its braided tail streaming behind her. In her wake, Maris and Halia grasp one another's flukes, spinning in a wheel until they blur, all definition lost in the flame of their streaming hair. They interweave their arms and press the oxygen tubes to one another's lips.

For centuries, sirens have ruled the vast and mysterious kingdom of the sea. The youngest does not share her sisters' contentment and longs for more. Her days have no distinguishing characteristics; they are dark with silt, and unchanging. She is weary of the sea's arctic cold. She is tired of half-light.

A shadow passes over Naia and she looks up, pantomiming wonder as fireworks shatter the surface, reflecting a celebration the likes of which the youngest siren has never seen.

Her sisters tell her no good can come of longing. Maris and Halia grasp her arms, beseeching her to stay with them. Galene holds tight to her tail. *But she pays them no heed. As she ventures toward the surface, the waves try to face her down, but she pushes on.*

The youngest siren reaches the line between sea and sky. The colors give way to rain that, from below, shimmers on the surface like stars. Lightning splits the sea and Nixie, in a prince's leggings and billowing white shirt, crashes into the sirens' kingdom, trailing a ribbon of blood.

The siren cannot bear to watch him drown. Ignoring her sisters, whose warnings are whipped away on the waves, she wraps her arms around the prince's waist. He opens his mouth and the sea pours in. His fingers tangle in her hair, dragging her down with him. Ceto, as the sea witch in glittering black, materializes in a crack of thunder with a shriek.

Ceto's rage is all-consuming. She channels it into her pantomimed scream and, even in its imagined vibration, it is the most primal sound she has uttered since giving birth. She is not vexed at Naia for what she cannot help, for what Ceto herself has passed along to her. But if she is anything like her mother, Naia will soon be impossible to control. The prospect of losing control terrifies Ceto—and fear infuriates her. Through years of self-discipline, she turns insecurity into anger. Ceto cannot punish her daughter for testing the limits of her influence, and yet she cannot allow it to happen again.

Fury flashes in the witch's eyes. Seething, she spins to the windows, baring her teeth at the audience, where a man has smashed his manhood snaillike against the window. She barely notices. This is not the first such incident; nor will it be the last. As the bartender twists the man's arm behind his back and peels him away from the glass, the sirens continue performing, unruffled.

Ceto forgets the man the minute the window is clear. She forgets everyone beyond the glass as soon as she turns away from them. The sea witch offers the siren magic for a price—the prince's life in exchange for her tail. The siren closes her eyes, weighing the value of one life against another. Then she thrusts her palm at the witch and turns her face away. The witch slashes her teeth across the siren's hand and lifts the prince's face to the gauze of blood. Air fills his lungs. He opens his eyes to the siren.

With a greedy smile, the witch slits the siren's tail from seam to fluke and peels away its sides. A white gown unfurls in its place, tangling around the siren's legs. Her chest constricts with sudden need, and the prince has become heavy in her all-too-human arms.

Aching for breath, the girl clasps the prince's hands and together they ascend toward the surface. But her sisters will not let her go. They clutch her gown, desperate to keep her below the sea. She scrabbles at their hands, her eyes pleading, losing her battle for air. The prince breaks from her grip and swims for the surface, abandoning the girl who saved him. The sirens' song rings across the sea.

Of her bones are coral made;

Those are pearls that were her eyes.

She raises her arms and fixes her dying gaze on the line between sea and sky as her final breath leaves her lungs. She drifts down to the black hole, tangled in her wedding dress.

Nothing of her that doth fade,

a sea-change into something rich and strange.

In their desire to keep her for themselves, her sisters have slain her as thoroughly as thrusting a blade through her heart.

• • •

The first time Ceto almost lost Naia was at her birth. Urgency had drawn her to her swollen feet. She'd vacuumed the house, scrubbed the toilet, and folded laundry into drawers, ignoring the ache blooming inside her.

When the pain overcame her, she'd curled onto her side in the front hall. Pressure ground into her center. She wrapped her arms around her stomach, where the child strained against her ribs and pelvis, filling its space.

The light from the front windows pooled around her, shifted over her, stroked her where she lay lost to her own ragged breath, until she could no longer bear to be contained. She crawled outside to the edge of the cornfield, craving the open air, groaning with pain that pinned her to the earth on her hands and knees.

The child wormed inside her, and the pain came in stormy waves. Rendered to base animal instinct, on all fours, Ceto gave in to her body. She bore down with untried muscles, shocking herself with her own guttural sounds. Mid-groan, she scolded herself, "Must you do that?"

Alone but for the crows accusing her from the rooftop, she was cleaved from the inside to make way for her child. It was a girl. And she was stillborn.

Powerless against the sobs that wracked her aching body, she slid the baby up her stomach. The spicy scent of blood was familiar and overpowering. The child was mottled purple; the cord wound around her neck. Ceto grappled with its chainlike rope, but it slipped in her fingers. In desperation, she gnawed through it and hoisted the child up by her ankles, pounding her back like the waves beating against the shore.

She'd once heard of an orca who had carried her dead calf for seventeen days in an aimless, grief-blind journey. Its anguish had been beyond Ceto's understanding until this moment as she pounded and pounded.

Her daughter gasped. She pulled up her knees and wailed, sending the crows shrieking over the cornfield. Ceto drew the baby to her chest, back to the bloody dirt.

She was stunned by her daughter's legs, purple and clotted with vernix like the rest of her. Ceto stroked her back, furred with a nearly imperceptible cloak of down. This child was a stranger yet so achingly familiar. It was her fishlike movements that had rippled down Ceto's belly, her spine that had pressed against Ceto's stretched flesh, her heels that had thumped Ceto's rib cage.

The intense physicality of her love for this child was different from the love she shared with her husband, expressed in the often-painful striving to fit their bodies together. This was something else.

As the infant quieted against her breast, the ferocity of Ceto's love turned her inside out. It made her want to die. She had been foolish to pursue this all-consuming feeling when life can be so easily extinguished.

In tearing from her mother's body, the child had riven a wound inside Ceto that cramped and bled with rawness she knew would never heal. Her daughter had begun moving away from her the minute she was born, and not even the vehemence of Ceto's love could close the distance between them. It pained her to think she would always love Naia more than her daughter would love her; that she would not comprehend the force with which she was loved until she was herself a mother. And then she would love her own child more than Ceto.

Ceto's loneliness returned stronger than before, even as she threw herself into motherhood. She was captivated by the warm, mousy smell of the top of Naia's head; the weight of her; how she waved her arms involuntarily like anemones and craned her neck, searching her world with unfocused eyes. Her eyesight, Ceto learned, was as poor as if she were gazing up at her mother's face through the bleary boundary between sea and sky.

Naia unfurled in water and spread her arms and legs to roll and flip as she had in the womb. In the vast nothingness of air, where there was no weight to push against, she contracted into herself again, pulling up her knees, her hands in fists. Her daughter's dexterity in water was the only trait Ceto found familiar. Naia was otherwise foreign to her.

In the milk-stained hours of half sleep, her rent body throbbing, Ceto awoke searching for her baby among the pillows. She slept with her ear pressed against Naia's chest. The nights were heavy with fear, and Ceto dreamt of all the ways her daughter could die. She could suffocate Naia in the crook of her arm. She could crack her skull against the wall or trip and toss her from a great height. Plagued by the compulsion to act on these visions, she'd given corners wide berth and clutched Naia to her chest when descending stairs. She'd scoffed at baptism but allowed it on the off-chance that it might protect her daughter's soul.

No matter how rigorously she held off catastrophe, Ceto lost her daughter in a million little ways that cut deep. She returned to work when Naia was two months old. Her husband promised he had a big project coming in soon, but until then, they needed her wages. Daycare will be good for the child, he said. But Naia screamed when taken from her mother's arms, and Ceto screamed on her way to work, her car windows rolled up tight.

Ceto thought about Naia during meetings and while pumping in the ladies' restroom under fluorescent lights. Her shirt was stained with milk. Her arms ached for Naia's weight. At five o'clock, she sped to daycare, her breasts hard, her heart squeezed in anticipation. She found Naia serene in her caregiver's arms. She should have been grateful, but jealousy consumed her.

The caregivers were the first to see Naia roll over. They knew her favorite songs and how to calm her when she cried. When Naia's teeth began cutting through her gums, the caregivers were the ones who comforted her. They described Ceto's daughter to her, as if they knew the child better than her own mother.

They advised Ceto to bathe Naia more often, coddle her less. She likes bananas, they said. She's constipated; feed her prunes. When Ceto stowed bottles of milk in the daycare fridge and leaned in to kiss Naia goodbye, her daughter turned away to nestle into her caregiver's neck.

Naia began to court self-destruction. She gummed small items she found on dirty floors. She slept on her stomach with her face pressed flat. She reached for strangers. Naia is a biter, her caregivers said. It's a problem they must work together to address. But Ceto was relieved her daughter could take care of herself.

She, too, longed to bite—to devour her colleagues who rushed up and down the hallways with jangling keys and shrill voices. When Naia bit while nursing, Ceto savored the pain. Naia was the only good that had come out of the experiment of marriage. For that alone, it was worth the self-obliteration. Yet no one could blame Ceto for what she did to reclaim herself.

Naia still sleeps with her arms thrown above her as if in surrender. She has twisted away from Ceto in the oyster shell. Her cheeks are flushed, her hair clings to her forehead. Ceto gently lowers her arms to her sides and hugs Naia closer inside their shell as if to press her back inside herself.

She knows she is cold. Sometimes she wishes she could be gentler, more affectionate, but her daughter must be tough to survive in this world. Coddling Naia would do her a disservice. Only when her daughter is sleeping does Ceto kiss her.

She counts the beats of Naia's heart as she has every night since her birth, fearing it might stop again. She listens for a change, for any indication that her daughter's heart has moved away from her.

4

Naia's strongwoman wheels her throne up the path that winds along the clifftop. At its highest point, a man paces on a platform extending out over the sea. He stops to watch her approach and waves with his whole arm, then yanks it down, as though embarrassed by his enthusiasm.

Naia works all the proposals. Nixie is scared of heights, and none of the others can pull off the suggestion of innocence required for romantic performances. Naia doesn't mind; she likes the spectacle of it, and the couples' hopefulness offers an alternative to her mother and aunts' jaded interpretation of love.

Ceto hasn't mentioned the kiss. Naia suspects her mother is devising a suitable punishment for her transgression. She should probably be afraid, but no punishment will be harsh enough for nearly drowning that boy—and enjoying it.

From this vantage point, Sirenland is smaller than it seems from within; the sea melds with the infinite horizon beyond the boundary of their kingdom. On the beach far below, a scattering of guests pick along the sand, their stilt-like shadows stretching toward the ocean.

Ceto lounges on the Sailor's Ruin, gazing off into some ever-receding world. Naia has never understood what her mother calls the sea's hypnotic draw. The sea is simply part of her. She knows it as well as her own body and would no sooner spend hours watching her own chest rise and fall.

The strongwoman sets Naia's throne before the iron railing that runs along the length of the cliff's edge. The man stands a few feet back, shifting in place with jittery anticipation. He doesn't *look* like someone Naia would need protection from.

"Sorry—I'm afraid of heights," he says and leans out to shake her hand. His palm is damp. The strongwoman growls a warning, and he jerks away.

"Sorry. I forgot the rules. I'm nervous. Thanks for doing this."

He has a nice face, Naia decides. His hair flops into his eyes, and she wishes she could push it back.

"Are you scared?" he asks.

"I do this all the time," she says, wanting to impress him.

The excitement in his eyes falters. Of course, he would want this gesture to be special, and she's just cheapened it.

"But each time is different," she adds. "And we've never had anyone say no."

"Here's hoping we don't buck the trend." He offers her a grateful but distracted smile, glancing over his shoulder at the porta-potties. The light blue of his eyes melts into the sky behind them.

He could be a character from the romances Naia steals from the beach but has never had the freedom to read.

The girl who emerges from the toilet is too short and plain to be a romantic heroine. Unafraid, she strides to the edge of the cliff and leans out over the railing, her hair slashing at her face.

The man closes his eyes, takes a breath, and joins her at the edge. He grips the railing as if he doesn't trust it. The woman kisses his cheek, and he offers her a smile that animates his whole face, utterly different from the one he'd presented to Naia a moment before. This was different even from the expressions of love the sirens pantomime in the theater, theirs a pale facsimile of the real thing. No one has looked at Naia like that, and she can't imagine anyone ever will. Her chest pinches with jealousy over what she's missing, and hadn't even known to want until this moment.

"How about a pearl?" the man asks his girlfriend, as if he's just thought of it.

"Really?" She claps in childlike delight.

He wraps his arm around her waist and turns her to Naia, who wears pearl-studded shells for the occasion. Her hair is bound in strands of pearls, and her fingers are heavy with pearl rings.

"'T'would be my pleasure," Naia says, according to the script. Sirens never allow their emotions to interfere with their work.

The strongwoman fits Naia's throne into the gate in the railing. She faces the sea, with nothing between her and the open sky. Her fluke flutters in the breeze. She embraces her body's need to launch into the air and the answering call of her earthbound blood beating it back.

She recites to the sky: *"Orient pearls fit for a queen / Will I give thy love to win, / And a shell to keep them in."*

She closes her eyes with a dramatic pause, as if gathering herself for a feat that defies nature. She counts to five along with the rhythm of her eager heart, sinking into the silence of the audience behind her, their held breath, their anticipation.

Naia tightens her muscles and launches from the throne. She imagines the couple reaching out to her as she dives with her palms outstretched, shattering the resistance of the air.

She pulls up her tail behind her with a shriek of joy, longing to kick it off and feel the air against her legs, to scissor them wildly and pinwheel in the sky like the children who jump off the boardwalk on summer nights. She parts the sea with her hands. It accepts her with relief.

Naia yields to the impact of the water along the length of her body. It flips her belly-down to the sand. Her tail catches the current and sweeps her toward the cove. When she finds equilibrium, she opens her eyes.

She knows this landscape more intimately than her own body. Each swell along the sea floor, each knoll of coral, establishes her place in Sirenland. Naia checks on her treasures tucked under the rock shelf and curbs her impulse to sort through the looted purse, deferring the pleasure until later when she'll have time to enjoy it.

She scouts along the craggy oyster reef for the largest, oldest shells, the ones reserved for Sirenland's big spenders. She could simply pluck any old oyster off the reef, of course—the guests don't know any better—but they're paying for spectacle. To some, she offers it freely. She withholds from others; the more demanding the client, the less effort she devotes to finding just the right pearl.

She wants a good one for this man. She'll hold her breath, keeping him in suspense as he leads the woman down to the beach. She'll let them wait, allow them time to enjoy a picnic and a glass of champagne.

Then, she'll ride the waves to shore, where she'll present the man with an oyster. She'll make sure it's a hairy one, coarse with seaweed and barnacles. The finest pearls are forged in the ugliest shells.

He'll accept the oyster from Naia's hands, turn to the woman, and drop to one knee. Naia's aunts will cheer, as if they didn't participate in weekly proposals, and pretend to celebrate a love they don't believe will last.

A proposal always reawakens Naia's curiosity about her father. The love she plays this role in securing is so different from the crude encounter her mother exploits as a cautionary tale. Her mother would have her believe that stepping out into the world without her tail, without her mother and aunts, would invite violation. But Naia doubts whether any man could overpower Ceto unless she invited the subjugation.

Naia skims her fingers over the ridge of shells, closed tight against her inspection, their edges sharp as knives to defend the soft muscle within. A crab scuttles away from her searching hands, revealing a perfect oyster. Naia pries it from its cluster. It fills her palm, certain to contain a plump pearl that will impress the man waiting on the beach. She pushes up from the sea floor to return to the surface—and collides with a body.

A girl hovers in the waves, her face blue-tinged and swollen. Her hair webs around her head. Tethered to the sea floor by a concrete block, she sways with the waves like a frond of bull kelp. Her polka-dotted bikini strains across her bloated skin. The oyster slices Naia's hand.

5

The second time Ceto almost lost Naia, it was her own fault. She'd arrived at Sirenland in a bloody dress seeking asylum and had instead found a defunct roadside attraction sagging with mold and despair. It had shut down years ago when a mermaid drowned during a show, in front of an audience of families with small children. No one wanted to vacation where women died.

Ceto moved into the office above the bar, clearing out the former owner's clutter except for a fold-out cot and a gold plaster throne. She'd pored over Sirenland's account books and detailed her plans for its resurrection. She worked into the early morning, and when she could no longer focus on numbers, she curled around Naia and fell into a dreamless sleep. Not even the infant's hungry cries could rouse her.

From the rooms of junk adjoining the tiled bunker, Ceto had salvaged strings of colored lights, paste jewelry, road signs, props, wigs, and five mirrors with stage lights. When one room was clear, she painted it bruised purple and mounted the mirrors along the wall. She painted the second room the dusky pink of an oyster shell.

Ceto repurposed the silicone tails she'd found on hooks in the bunker and rasped mildew from the tiled floor. The tube was so choked with scum that she spent a week digging through it until her fingernails turned black. With Naia safely tucked into a lobster trap behind the bar, Ceto scraped a decade's worth of algae from the observation window until the glass was clear as the water. Then, she bolted the old road signs back along the highway and roped a banner promising "Live Mermaids!" between the utility poles down the road.

She began by advertising Sirenland to the nearby naval base, whose sailors wouldn't care that a woman had died here. She crafted a persona to entice them—a beautiful and ferocious siren tamed by a prince's love. The sailors wanted her—and she needed the sailors, although she told herself she was using them. She built Sirenland with their money and crafted her perception of herself through the mirror of their gaze.

Only in performing could she forget about the audience and the transactional relationship she was obliged to cultivate. Released from the weight of gravity, she could feel her muscles lengthening. The languorous movement was a welcome change from the frenetic pace of life on land where her every action was fraught. In the spring, she forgot the limitations of her humanity.

Addicted to the rush, Ceto added more shows and introduced

Naia into the performances. People began traveling from miles around to see Ceto and the Aquatic Infant, as she came to be known.

Naia drew families with small children who pressed their hands against the glass, and even sailors softened at the sight of her as she flipped and rolled past the windows. She petted the hairy rocks at the rim of the black hole, rode the current that picked her up like strong arms and bore her grinning through the seagrass. She rivaled Ceto in the length of time she could dance without drawing breath.

After each show, Ceto stripped off her daughter's tail and sponged her legs and the crevice between them. She powdered Naia's folds and furrows so they wouldn't chafe. She longed to taste the plump loaves of Naia's limbs.

The child did not take calmly to this new life. She thrashed as Ceto bound her in her tail. She stroked Ceto's face, then struck without warning. She awoke just as Ceto was drifting to sleep and refused to lie still. She screamed unless carried in her mother's arms that were already numb from performing. Ceto gave her daughter everything, but Naia demanded more of her, and still more.

Ceto tried to appoint the one-armed bartender as night nurse, but he shied away from Naia's body, its softness and vulnerability. He refused to change her, averting his eyes from her center.

"It's just not right," he said. "Seeing her opened up like that, like a gutted fish."

Heavy-eyed, Ceto lost her way in the tank; forgot and tried to breathe, only to rise up the tube choking with humiliation. The audience laughed at her confusion. The sailors' gaze, absent of desire, no longer sustained the version of herself she had forged. She became aware of the sagging skin under her arms and the way her stomach jutted above her tail seam. Ceto asked the bartender why he never tried to fuck her. Of course, she's beautiful, he said, but she is also a mother. Ceto added a late-night show and danced alone.

In the early mornings when she retired, spent, she found Naia asleep with tears dried to salt on her cheeks. She told herself she was doing everything for her daughter. But at only six months old, Naia couldn't appreciate her sacrifices.

Ceto was lonelier than she'd been in the cornfields beneath the bald sky. And more useless. She could barely perform. She could not meet her daughter's needs. She was riven between warring roles she was not enough to fill. Only Naia remained blissfully innocent of her mother's failures. And yet, Ceto carried on the business of creating her mythology. What else could she do?

There was always work to be done, much of it thankless and often distasteful. She derived no pleasure from conferring with the cook on bar food she couldn't eat, or settling the accounts, although they were finally balanced and even thriving. And she loathed her weekly trips away from Sirenland to the nearby docks, where she was seen as a customer rather than a queen. She strode barefoot through pools of seawater glistening on the boards, heedless of the guts beneath her heels. Naia was strapped to her chest, sleeping for once.

The sun would not rise for another hour, but the dock was swarming with movement. The fishermen did not give her a second glance as she passed the ships from which they hauled streaming nets of fish onto the boards. She was equally invisible to the forklift operators stacking pallets and lobster traps. Not even the gulls noticed her as they blizzarded above the ships and weathered pilings, eyeing the morning's catch.

At the end of the dock, the fishmonger in his orange bib overalls and rubber boots lorded over the fish he'd laid out on a bed of ice for her scrutiny. A neat row of snapper stared walleyed at the lightening sky. On hooks behind him, four swordfish hung from their tails, dripping blood on the boards below.

Ceto unstrapped Naia from her chest and settled her on the dock in a semicircle of barrels chattering with blue crabs, quahog clams, spiny lobsters. The child was sleeping, her hands tucked in fists beneath her chin. It was the first time in three days Naia hadn't awoken upon being set down. Ceto swayed with fatigue, but she had no time for rest.

The fishmonger reached elbow-deep into a tub at his feet and pulled out a shining king mackerel, expounding on its torpedo shape. He likened it to a fancy car, built for speed, and moved on to a cooler of scallops, dandling their plump flesh the way he might a woman's breasts.

Ceto understood the necessity of maintaining relationships

with her vendors, which meant listening to this man explain the difference between mackerel and mullet. And yet, her feet stung and her back was tender from the straps of Naia's sling, and she was so very tired. As the fishmonger droned on, her eyes slid shut against her will, and his voice began to take on a dreamlike quality.

"And here, a beautiful grouper, sweet and light with a firm texture reminiscent of—" the fishmonger was saying. The effrontery of it jolted her awake.

"You expect my child to eat bottom-feeders?" Ceto glanced over her shoulder at Naia to punctuate her displeasure. The child was gone. Seagulls screamed above the dock.

Ceto's first thought was that a gull had stolen Naia and smashed her like a mollusk on the beach. Her hand flew to her mouth in a parody of terror that she knew was a parody, even as she pressed her fingers against her lips. For one nightmarish moment, the line between reality and performance blurred.

The fishmonger followed her gaze across the dock where Naia was crawling along the salt-buckled boards. She reached for a faint square of shadow, as if testing the temperature of pool water, and pulled herself into it.

The shadow was cast by a refrigerator-size tub of fish straining its straps as a crane lowered it to the dock. Naia looked up.

The fishmonger shouted and bound forward in his rubber boots. He tumbled to his knees and wedged beneath the tub, hauling Naia out from under the load just as it shuddered to the dock.

The fishmonger clutched Naia to his chest. She screeched and twisted to bite his thick fingers, but he gripped her tighter, his breath rasping. The crane operator scrambled out of his seat and stared at them openmouthed as Ceto wrested Naia away from the fishmonger, muffling her daughter's wails against her breast.

"Jesus!" the fishmonger said. "She was almost crushed."

"She wasn't," Ceto snapped, trembling with the panic that had gripped her like a wild animal.

"Are you crazy, bringing a baby here?" the crane operator demanded, his face white.

Ceto shook her head, squeezing Naia so hard the child screamed. She pushed past the men, who stepped aside as if afraid of her. Naia could have died because of her, because she couldn't keep her eyes open, because she was a bad mother.

Ceto ran past the rows of fish, heedless of the puddles pink with blood. Gristle sliced her feet, but she didn't notice the pain. She wasn't enough; could never be enough for Naia. The realization confirmed her primal fear: that the responsibility of motherhood was too great, the potential loss of her child too painful, to endure. If she couldn't be a good mother, she would have to find Naia a better one.

• • •

Alone in her dressing room, Ceto cradles her blistered hands.

Her arms burn from dragging the girl and her ballast out to sea. Sirenland could not survive another death.

She slides down in her throne to rest her head against one gilded wing and closes her eyes. Naia had known better than to say anything in front of the happy couple. She had presented the pearl. The man had proposed, and the girl had accepted. It was only later, in the privacy of the dressing room, that Naia had told her mother what she'd found, unblinking with horror.

A soft knock sounds on the dressing room door.

"Enter." Ceto's voice is hoarse from calling to the sharks.

Galene slips inside. Her nightdress hides her legs. With the ease of long habit, Galene withdraws to the adjoining bathroom to fill the pail under the sink and retrieves the sponge from the hook.

Ceto leans back on the throne as Galene runs her fingers along her seam and rolls her tail down her thighs. It leaves a bite mark around her waist where the flesh is thicker than it had once been.

"What did you do with the girl?" Galene asks, tugging the tail down over her knees. Ceto points her toes so Galene can yank it free.

"No one will find her," Ceto says, averting her eyes from her center.

When immersed in Sirenland's mythology, she can believe herself to be separate from and loftier than other women. But in these private moments, stripped of her tail, she is reminded of the reality beneath the fantasy. Her human vulnerability is what makes her ferocity acceptable to an audience.

"Poor thing," Galene says, her voice wavering with unshed tears. She hangs Ceto's tail on a hook, beside the dry one Ceto will put on as soon as she is clean.

Galene skims the sponge over Ceto's feet and calves, as she has every day for the last fourteen years. She squeezes the sponge into the bucket and runs it up between Ceto's legs. Water rolls down her chafed skin. Galene presses her lips between Ceto's thighs.

It brings Ceto pleasure despite herself. She resents her body for its vulnerability, yet succumbing to it grants her pleasure. Galene is the only person she allows herself to be vulnerable with, and only sometimes.

Ceto guides Galene's head away. She slides her hand inside Galene's nightdress, gathering one heavy breast in her palm. She prefers touching to being touched, forcing Galene to surrender rather than surrendering herself.

"Are you all right?" Galene asks, pressing herself more firmly into Ceto's hand.

Ceto nods, and even that small gesture sends ropes of pain down her weary shoulders.

"The sea heals all wounds," she says, reassuring Galene, and herself. "We will find peace in performing."

"But—" Galene gasps as Ceto rolls her nipple between her fingers and shifts away. "We won't be performing for a while."

Ceto looks at her blankly and Galene explains with infinite patience, "The girl is missing—there's an investigation. Police are combing the boardwalk and the Coast Guard has closed the beach. There's no audience."

Ceto hears the words but they don't sink in. How could there not be an audience? She had taken care of the girl.

She struggles to stand, but Galene places her hands on her thighs, pressing her back onto the throne.

"I'll handle it," she says. "You took care of the child; let me handle the rest. I'll talk to the police and reporters. I'll go on the news if I have to, and say how sorry we are for the family, how nothing like this has ever happened here and never will again. But we need to think of Naia above all."

Ceto should be grateful. She should be glad Naia and Galene have a strong bond, one she has encouraged all these years. She *is* grateful, but she is also jealous. Galene is the mother Naia deserves.

Fifteen years ago, she had answered Ceto's ad for a nanny and arrived at Sirenland, then as Dolores, with her eyes downcast at her orthopedic shoes, her hands twisting in the skirt that draped to her knees.

"Do you have children?" Ceto had asked.

Dolores smoothed the skirt against her thighs, leaving damp streaks along the fabric.

"My child died before taking a breath," she said, her voice quiet but steady.

Ceto scoured her face for grief or rage or desperation, but there was nothing written there. The only betrayal of emotion was a tightening of her jaw. Ceto felt she should say, "I'm sorry," but she wasn't sorry; she was relieved it was Dolores's child and not her own.

Ceto studied her wide hips and chapped hands and heavy breasts. She wondered what Dolores tasted like. It was the first time she had felt desire since the earliest days with her husband. She'd hired Dolores as much for Naia as for herself.

If Naia so much as sighed in the night, Dolores swept into the bedroom to gather her up. She changed and rocked her until she was calm. She gave Naia a frozen washcloth as her teeth ripped through her swollen gums. She introduced songs and games to help Naia develop fine motor skills. She folded Naia's hands around her own fingers and guided her across the room on unsteady legs. These developments were alien to Ceto. The less she related to her daughter's evolution, the less connected she felt to Naia, and she had clung to her in ways she did understand, pulling her close at night.

On what would be their final outing together—and the last time Ceto would leave her dressing room without her tail—Dolores spread a picnic blanket on the beach, humming the Ferris wheel tune to Naia who played in the sand beside her. The dress Ceto had worn when she'd arrived at Sirenland now gaped at her neck and under her arms. Performing had carved away her curves.

Naia dropped fistfuls of sand onto the blanket, dusting the tuna Dolores had prepared for lunch. As she tested her evolving agency, Naia spoiled everything she touched.

"Stop that." Ceto squeezed her daughter's fist until the sand drained from between her fingers. The child's face turned stormy, heralding another tantrum that only Dolores could calm.

Dolores hoisted Naia into her arms and slid her soft hand into Ceto's. Although the meat of her palm was tender, her grip was strong, and she spun Naia out of her temper until she squealed. Her innocent joy surprised Ceto into laughter.

Naia took her first independent steps on the beach that day, reaching out to the Ferris wheel. Ceto and Dolores chased her, hand in hand. They led her on with shining objects, shells, sunlight on the waves.

Ceto had thought they were happy. She'd thought they finally had everything they needed, until the night Dolores waded through the ocean of the bedroom and slipped into the oyster shell. Ceto shifted to face her, studying her solemn eyes, her chapped lips. Their arm hairs rose toward one another in the dark.

"I'm ready," Dolores whispered.

"For what?" Ceto asked, half-dozing still.

Dolores brushed her fingers against Ceto's.

"I want to be like you."

Ceto awoke fully to the anger coursing through her. She'd turned away every woman who had begged for sirenhood, college girls seeking summer jobs, bored housewives craving excitement, and all the silly girls who'd hoped a tail could lure a man down the aisle. Sirenhood is not a whim; it is a way of life, she'd scolded them as she'd sent them on their way.

"Is that why you came to Sirenland?" she asked, dreading the answer.

"Yes." Dolores wove her fingers through Ceto's and squeezed. "I wanted—I *hoped*—to transform. That's why I came, but it's not why I've stayed. I love you and Naia."

Ceto glared at the ceiling, glowing pink like the inside of a shell. None of the other women who'd come to her in search of sirenhood had been prepared to commit, to offer her the absolute fealty she commanded. None had possessed the combination of fortitude and pliability required to remake themselves in her image.

"I want to stay however you'll have me," Dolores said. "Please, just think about it."

"This is not a whim," she snapped.

Naia stirred against her side, and Dolores rubbed between her shoulder blades, soothing her back to sleep. Since Dolores had arrived, Ceto's loneliness had receded. Dolores had adopted the role of sister and performed with affection Ceto's own sisters had never shown her. She was more passionate than Ceto's husband had been, and more devoted.

Ceto was softening against her will. Dolores had made Sirenland a home. Ceto could create a family to inhabit it.

"Sirenhood is for life," she said. "There is no going back."

"I don't want to go back," Dolores said, simply. Her voice was steady, her hand playing unhurried across Naia's spine.

Ceto had to be certain. The risk to all she'd built was too great to allow even the slightest doubt through the cracks she was striving to seal with her own sweat and blood. She'd seen the ruin doubt could unleash. Any challenge to its fragile reality would bring Sirenland crashing down around them. Dolores must place her trust in Ceto and the world she had created—and fully accept it as her reality.

Ceto eased away from the sleeping child and pressed up on her palms above Dolores. She traced one finger along her cheek and followed its path with her lips, down the slide of Dolores's chin and into the dip of her throat.

"I will hurt you," Ceto whispered against her hot skin.

"Please," Dolores whispered back, lying still beneath her. Only her breath betrayed her, coming quicker as Ceto slid her teeth into her neck, meeting vein.

Dolores's blood was sweet and musky, heady as Ceto imagined her knee creases would taste, or her underarms. Her aching need for Sirenland was as tart as Ceto's own, proving her worthiness. Ceto had brought her here for Naia—but she'd keep Dolores for herself.

Sensing the boundary she'd learned not to cross, Ceto tore her teeth from Dolores's tender skin. She had long ago mastered her hunger.

Dolores became her first siren, reborn Galene. As intimately as Ceto would come to know her, Galene remained a tantalizing mystery. There was something else in her blood, a withheld secret, an acerbic fear that coated the back of Ceto's tongue. That's good, Ceto had thought; fear binds stronger than love.

Ceto has lived with fear for so long it had settled into a familiar burn behind her eyes—but the girl's death and the invasion of the outside world into her own has given it a different quality, a bite that takes Ceto's breath away.

"What do we do about Naia?" Galene sits back on her heels, searching out Ceto's gaze with damp eyes. Her face is like a wound. The fear in her voice ignites Ceto's own, fanning it up her chest so she can barely breathe.

"What *about* Naia?" she asks.

"We don't know what happened to the girl. If someone *killed* her—" Galene chokes on the word.

Anguish flames up Ceto's throat, but she will not betray this vulnerability, even to Galene.

"Do you doubt I can protect Naia—and you all?" she asks. "You are safe here."

They had to be. If they could be hurt *here*, a haven she'd spent every waking moment securing, then nowhere was safe.

Galene grasps Ceto's knees as if to anchor herself against a coming storm.

"Of course, I don't doubt you, but some things are beyond even your control."

"Nothing is beyond my control."

"You can't possibly—" Galene's voice catches, deepens like a chain unspooling into a dark rift in the sea floor. "Naia is never going to forget what she's seen. It will change her in ways we can't anticipate or understand. She's going to need help."

"That is what *you* are for."

Galene looks at her blankly, lost in her own depths as if the chain had broken.

"From someone trained to help," Galene insists. "I would protect Sirenland with my life, but Naia needs—"

"You don't know what she needs." Ceto's voice is tight with anger, but Galene digs deeper.

"I raised that girl," she says. "I defer to you in all things but this."

"*You* are not her mother," Ceto snaps, as blood wells beneath Galene's fingernails and slides warm down the backs of her legs.

"I'm more her mother than you are." Galene holds Ceto's gaze despite the pulse jumping at her throat. She knows better than to challenge Ceto. She knows the risk she is taking.

Rage clouds Ceto's vision, warring with pride. She wants Galene to be strong—but she must also be subservient. The balance of power at Sirenland hangs on Ceto's authority. She draws the chill of the ocean into her voice. She knows what she's doing and does it anyway, enunciating every word:

"Your child is dead. Do not tell me what to do with mine."

Galene's cheeks redden as if she's been slapped. She tears her nails from Ceto's knees and lurches to her feet, pulling her nightdress across her breasts.

"I will handle the authorities, and I will talk to Naia, since that is what I'm *for*," Galene says. "But from now on you will wash your own damn cunt."

Galene strides to the door, her body straining to run. *Good for Dolores; standing up for herself at last.* Ceto allows herself a moment of angry satisfaction as the door slams shut, and thinks, *I made that.*

6

The Coast Guard closes the beach, dredging the sea up to the net barrier. The girl's parents clutch one another as the police confer with them, as reporters follow them up the coast to the boardwalk where the search extends beyond Naia's sight. The girl's brother trails behind them. The surliness he had shared with his sister has dulled into perpetual dread.

Watching the broken family shuffle up the beach, Naia wonders what her mother did with the girl, but she would never ask. She understands that the sanctity of this place depends on its veneer of magic, the guests' perception that Sirenland is a kingdom apart from reality, a place of escape where mermaids exist and bad things do not. But the cost of maintaining this myth seems too great when weighed against a grieving family.

Salt is everywhere. It cakes into the creases of Naia's body, under her nails, in her knuckles, under her arms. Galene rubs lotion into her skin, but her joints are still dry and cracked. Filling her lungs requires extra effort. It becomes ever more difficult to resist the drag of the sea, as if having claimed one girl's life, it yearns for another.

Naia wades up through the gloom of sleep to the oyster shell, awoken by her own cries. She turns away from Ceto and curls around the strange fear blooming inside her chest. Her mother presses her lips to the back of Naia's neck.

Ceto has warned her not to say anything to her aunts, as if Naia would want to talk about it. As if she'd want to think about it. If she could scrub the memory from her mind, she would—but the image of the girl's bloated face is there, always behind her eyelids, *her bones are coral made, a sea-change into something rich and strange.* The wavering lines of song come back to her in an unceasing refrain. *Sea-nymphs hourly ring her knell: Ding-dong—ding-dong—*

With the park closed, there is nothing to do. Naia stays in bed, tossing fitfully, *ding-dong, ding-dong, ding-dong* until she thinks it may just drive her mad.

Galene tries to get her to talk about what she saw and how she feels and what she needs, but Naia just gazes up at the ceiling until Galene slips out again. Naia's body aches for sleep; her eyelids are gritty, but she forces them to stay open so she doesn't have to see it again. *Ding-dong, ding-dong, ding-dong,* she feels like a rung bell.

• • •

Ceto hasn't gone a day without performing in fourteen years, and she's not about to start now. There may not be an audience, but the sea is eternal. She gathers her sirens to perform for the empty bar.

They are listless, executing the motions of the show at half pace, missing their cues. They suck from the hoses as if they cannot get enough air. Ceto feels it too, the unfamiliar constriction in her chest, the mechanical nature of her movements. She performs as if in a fog, pushing herself, and her sirens, to practice harder and for longer than usual. But it's no use. They need the audience to convince them of their reality.

She hears them bickering through the walls, catches snatches of whispered conversations tight with worry. They doubt the sanctity of Sirenland. They doubt Ceto.

Galene maintains their routines, ordering meals at the usual times, leading them to the tank at performance hours, turning out the lights at bedtime. She calms them with normality Ceto has never been able to embody, and had long ago given up striving for. Her husband had been charmed by what he called her quirks. Her formal speech, her inability to make small talk, her tendency to pour salt over every dish. He had laughed and kissed her forehead. Until now, she had never felt more trapped than by his love.

As she sits day after day in her throne, waiting for the storm of the girl's disappearance to pass, Ceto feels as she had then, surrounded by empty fields, when there was nothing to look forward to, and she had been no one.

Galene reads the papers so Ceto doesn't have to and shares the highlights tersely, like jabs to the ribs. The reporters cover the disappearance, but with no leads, they speculate, digging into the family's cracks. The father has a temper; perhaps he snapped, the papers suggest but never quite say. The brother likes violent video games, the mother hadn't let her date. The mother had been getting a massage when her daughter disappeared. The mother hadn't noticed she was gone for hours. The mother should have noticed, shouldn't she have?

The mother sits by the shore staring out to sea as if waiting for an answering tug from its depths. The fortune teller from the boardwalk sits beside her, holding her hand. They close their eyes and try to feel for the girl.

None of this matters Ceto says; the girl is gone. Galene just glares at her with that drowned-well look as if accusing her of being unnaturally cold, but Ceto never pretended to be otherwise.

• • •

Naia's aunts trade newspapers, poring over the details of the investigation and theorizing in hushed voices. Naia keeps her secret, protecting her aunts from the truth, although there is no one to protect her from it in return. Their gossip is infuriating. As much as they indulge in speculation, would they truly want to know about the concrete block or the girl's empty eye sockets or her bloated stomach? Her aunts can't possibly grasp the full horror of the girl's disappearance from newspapers. For Naia, it's visceral.

She learns that the girl's name was Claire Lewis and she was almost sixteen. These facts return some humanity to the wreck she had become. During the late-night shows, Naia steals the papers from Galene's drawer, scouring the pages for details that distance Claire Lewis from her tragic end.

She reads interviews with Claire's friends and selections from the diary she'd left under her hotel pillow, stuffed with poetry about her brother's best friend. The reporters share laundry lists of details: she'd ridden horses and wanted to be a dentist like her father. She got mostly A's except in gym. She'd been planning her sixteenth birthday party, a sleepover at a posh hotel.

Claire Lewis had been more than a victim or a mean girl in a bikini; she'd had plans and friends and a future. She'd wanted so much out of the life that was ripped from her, and as sad as Naia is for her, she pities herself more. Claire's death proves that life is short and precious, and Naia has been prevented from living hers for too long.

The papers run out of scavenged details and people tire of reading the same facts retold in different ways. Even the fortune teller seems bored by the mother's endless requests to retrace their steps once more, just one more time, try touching that rock, did we try that one there, do you sense anything, anything at all? She packs up her crystals and returns to the boardwalk. The police are called away to a homicide at a motel down the strip.

The Coast Guard departs to rescue a boat of drunken revelers. The guests flood back to the boardwalk, back to the beach, back to the bar.

The cries of the spectators follow Naia into the black hole beyond their sight. She holds herself in the mouth of the vent until their unease peaks—then she soars upward astride a plaster seahorse streaming bubbles in its wake. Naia waves to the audience.

She wants to vomit through her beguiling yet innocent smile. This fantasy seems awful now, a parody of true tragedy. That girl's death is the only real thing to have happened at Sirenland—and no one cares. The show goes on as before. As before, guests drink beyond the glass and the sirens perform as if nothing happened. *She* performs as if nothing happened.

The siren rides beyond her sisters' grasp to seize the prince. Together, they pierce the line between sea and sky and disappear from the spectators' view, into the tube concealed within the conch shell. A screen descends into the tank and a film is projected there: The prince extends his hand to the siren, now a maiden. They dance and, dancing, fall in love.

Concealed by the rocks, the sea witch gnashes her teeth and shakes her fists. As the prince leans in to kiss the siren, the witch shoots up through the tank in a swarm of bubbles and into the conch shell. She blasts onscreen, through the floor between the couple. The siren opens her mouth to scream but no sound emerges. The witch strikes her across the legs with her trident, and the siren sinks in a puddle of gown.

The screen retracts as the siren plunges into the tank, her regrown tail bound in the tulle of her wedding dress. The witch and the prince hurtle after her, battling for dominance, until the witch grasps the siren's hair like reins and drags her into the black hole. The prince follows them into the earth.

The music dies. The spectators hold their breath.

The siren's sisters gather at the mouth of the hole. They lock hands and bow their heads to sing:

O fair prince, handsome and free,
He loved a maid, his wife she'd be:
"O fair prince, come bide with me!"

As the tune fades into the waves, the spectators sag in their seats. The sirens tether themselves to one another against the current.

Then, in a cacophony of cymbals and drums, the prince ascends from the black hole, hauling the sea witch by the hair. She tears at him with her claws until his face is riven with gashes. The siren sails behind them, straining to reach the witch, but her sisters hold her back as the prince battles for her soul.

The siren snaps at their hands and arms with her teeth, forcing them to release her one by one, until only her eldest sister prevails. Just when Naia and Galene are meant to share an anguished glance and join the prince in defeating the sea witch, Galene's hand goes limp in Naia's. She begins to choke, her chest buckling, her gaze fixed on the window where a man pounds his fist on the glass. His mouth is open and the tendons in this neck bulge rope-like. Naia has seen plenty of men pressed against the window and this one seems no different than the rest. The bartender materializes behind him, pinning his arms behind his back. Galene's face is turning blue.

Ceto improvises. She impales the prince with her trident and grasps Galene around the waist, hauling her toward the tube with a triumphant laugh. She has exchanged one siren for another.

As the bartender hog-steps the man away, Naia tamps down her confusion and follows her mother's lead. She buries her face in her hands, collapsing in Maris and Halia's arms as the witch absconds with Galene into the conch shell. Nixie, in the prince's tattered white shirt, drifts down through the tank.

"O fair prince, come bide with me!"
But the prince now sleeps beneath the sea.

Galene quakes in Ceto's arms on the floor of the bunker, her face white beneath her makeup. The others kneel around them, stroking her hair and murmuring reassurances as if she were a child.

Men have tried to interrupt the show before, and Galene had taken it in stride. The stress of the investigation, her obsession with the newspapers, Galene's own loss—Ceto hadn't considered how hard this must have been for her.

"What is it?" Ceto whispers, cradling Galene's jaw in her palm. The others look on with wet, worried eyes.

Galene jerks away as if stung. Color floods back into her cheeks, flaming with barely controlled rage. She lifts her chin to meet Ceto's gaze.

"Nothing the sea can't heal," she snaps. Galene pushes up to her knees, her tail flopped beneath her like a crumpled train. "It won't happen again."

Halia and Maris press closer, folding her between them. Nixie doesn't touch them, but her face is pinched with uncertainty. And Naia, watching them all in silence, tries to hold herself impassive as the sea, but fear ripples across her face. They are all cracking.

And so is she. But Ceto cannot reveal weakness. She has a role to play; they all do. She rises above the sirens and arranges her face into a mask of authority.

"See that it doesn't," she says.

The Coast Guard may have retreated, but the bubble around Sirenland has been punctured. Ceto can feel it in the way the sirens avoid her gaze and press together in the tank and on the beach. Doubt has embedded here among them, in Galene's dread, in Naia's silence, and threatens to tear Sirenland apart from the inside. Ceto knows how to hide bodies and tame men and take what she wants. But this threat is invisible and insidious. She does not know how to fight it.

7

Naia awakens to the tail end of a scream, uncertain if it's hers. Its vibration hums in the air. Ceto's arms are tight around her, and she's glued to her mother with sweat. When as a child Naia had awoken in the night, Ceto had slept uninterrupted by her cries, lost in the current of her dreams. She sleeps that deeply still. Naia's heart pounds against her mother's ribs.

How can Ceto be so untouched by what has happened here? Naia's eyes ache. Her skin burns along the length of her mother's body. She untangles from Ceto, gasping for breath, and rips at the waistband of her too-tight tail in desperation as it slips through her shaking fingers. Finally, she finds purchase and tugs it violently down her thighs. She kicks it across the bed.

Naia slips into the seawater surrounding the oyster shell, welcoming the chill that engulfs her calves. The water slides around her in oily rings as she presses toward the steps that descend into the sea. She has never ventured alone from the sirens' chambers at night, and if her mother awakens to find her gone, Naia will lose more than a toe for this transgression.

She swims through the cliff tunnel, compelled by the need to escape from this suffocating, grief-sodden world where Claire lost her life and Naia has never been afforded the chance to live. Her breath comes short, even as she traverses the tunnel she knows by heart. She has no plan beyond escaping the cliffs.

The cove is empty in the moonlight. The sand stretches to the ocean like a swath of dun-colored fabric. Even the waves are silent, intensifying Naia's sense that the world has gone pale and lifeless.

The sea holds its breath as she swims along the cliff wall to the fissure in the limestone where she'd stowed the fishmonger's bag. Reassured by its heft, she slings it over her shoulder and rides the waves to shore.

There, she unfolds the top of the bag and unzips the opening. Pink fabric froths out onto the sand. Claire's dress and towel still hold her bug spray scent, now with a moldy tang. It dredges up Naia's longing for friendship, her bitter humiliation upon being rejected, her horror upon discovering Claire's bloated body. Pity brings tears to her eyes. Naia scrubs her skin with the towel, as if scouring the emotion from her body.

Relishing the sensation of cotton against her belly, she runs her palms down the plane of her stomach and the ledge of her pelvis, wondering at the way her legs connect to her torso, the joints and muscles she rarely has the opportunity to explore. There is no seam, no separation between bodies.

When she is fully dry, she slides the dress over her head. The material strokes her breasts and floats around her hips. The hem sweeps her thighs, exposing her long legs. She tests the weight of her body on land, the drag of her limbs and the strain of her muscles as she counters gravity to stand.

A hot breeze sails through the cove, carrying with it the music of the Ferris wheel. Far from the empty beach, the lights of the boardwalk promise excitement and warmth and life. Naia had always imagined leaving Sirenland would be physically impossible, as if it were surrounded by an invisible barrier that would hurl her back to her mother's kingdom where she belonged. She had never even tried.

Claire's purse holds a hair tie, two twenty-dollar bills, and a tube of strawberry-flavored lip gloss. The wallet that has fallen open on the sand reveals her driver's license. There are her freckles and sandy hair and stout features. Naia's memory of the girl blurs between her needful face and the ruin that became of her.

Her eyes were green, and she was five-foot-two. The photo is badly lit, highlighting Claire's blotchy skin and head-lit smile, as if the camera had flashed before she could arrange her face.

Naia watches herself apply the lip gloss in a compact engraved with Claire's initials. She shivers at this intimacy with the dead girl's lips. Claire had refused Naia's friendship, but now they are bound in death. Together, they head for the boardwalk.

• • •

Ceto awakens to an absence of sound, a barren call her senses are incapable of interpreting. The shell is empty beside her.

"Naia?" she cries out. In the retreating haze of sleep, she sees the drowned girl's swollen face, the rope sawing her flesh from bone, Naia's wounded eyes. Where is her daughter? Panic rushes through her body so fast and thick she gags on it.

The yawning call intensifies, and Ceto scrambles out of the shell, her heart thrashing against her ribs. The saltwater sharpens the command, hauling her out to the cove.

She rises to the surface and screams "Naia!" but there is no answer, except a stronger tug toward the open ocean.

Naia has never ventured out that far on her own—but the singing in Ceto's blood tows her into the deeper sea. She blinks away the vision of the girl's poor face and presses against Sirenland's barrier. Two figures waver in the gloom beyond the netting. She squints through the mud stirred up by her tail, straining to bring them into focus.

They push branchlike fingers through the barrier, their nails curved like eagle talons, brandishing their tails behind them. Their breasts are bare. They leer at her, exposing their daggered teeth. She rises to the surface gasping for breath, and they rise with her.

"How well you look, sister," they say in unison. Their eyes have no whites to lend them humanity. They are the opaque black of shark eyes.

"Where is my daughter?" Ceto demands, pulling her dignity around herself like a worn cloak. Fear for Naia overrides all else; she cannot know how she might have felt upon reuniting with her sisters otherwise. She hadn't allowed herself to imagine such a moment.

"That scrap of humanity?" Their voices seethe with contempt.

She follows their gaze to the clifftop where Naia strides against the night sky. Lit by the moon, the clouds have taken on the sickly glow of a gathering storm. A dress hugs her human curves and reveals her legs, an affront to her ancestry. Ceto's relief curdles into humiliation that her sisters are witness to her daughter's betrayal.

They laugh with the sound of splintering bone. "She obeys no better than her mother."

• • •

Captivated by the boardwalk lights and tinny music of the Ferris wheel and the laughter of a distant crowd, Naia passes over the clifftop where she dives for pearls and strikes out beyond the furthest point she'd ever ventured.

The boardwalk had always seemed to exist just out of reach. Even as she moves toward its lights, they appear to retreat from her. She is awkward on land, deprived of the grace for which she is known in the sea. She can't remember ever having walked on the beach, but as she pushes herself into a stumbling jog, the sensation of the sand caving beneath her heels is vaguely familiar. She propels forward against the drag of gravity, faster and faster until she is running toward the lights.

At last, planks emerge from the sand, the beginning of the boardwalk. The beach recedes at the base of an archway flaming with colored bulbs. Beyond it, the boardwalk swarms with families and strolling couples and racing teens. Vendors bellow from stalls with striped awnings, their depths glittering with ornaments and shell necklaces and gauzy dresses and wind chimes of frosted sea glass. Spinning teacups smear lights into the darkness. At the boardwalk's distant end, the Ferris wheel revolves against the sky. Its music is as familiar to Naia as the waves. The surrounding sea is so dark that the boardwalk could be anywhere, lifted out of space and time.

Since she was a child, Naia had gazed at the lights and longed to understand the mystery of what happened here. Now that she's finally found her way to the boardwalk, she is surprised by how easy it was to escape Sirenland. Returning will be much more difficult. For now, she won't think about what would happen if she were caught.

Naia loses herself in the bustle of the crowd, the cacophony of voices, the color and collision of bodies. She spins in place, wanting to do everything at once.

"Say cheese," someone orders, pressing her by the shoulders

into a stop. A woman raises an old-fashioned camera and snaps her photograph. Naia pulls closer to watch as the woman threads the picture into a plastic telescope attached to a keychain.

She presses her eye to the keyhole, and the photograph inside grows as if through a magnifying glass, revealing her standing against a tent, her face shining with heat. For all that Naia has posed and danced for cameras, this is the first photograph she's ever seen of herself. The guests who'd taken her picture had always taken it with them.

She squints at the girl in the keychain, searching out the person she sees in her aunts' mirrors. But that Naia is gone, replaced with a stranger who would be indistinguishable from any other girl baking on a beach towel. She is struck by the sight of her own long legs emerging from the bell of the dress and their paleness against the vibrant tent. Studying this version of Naia, walking with her eye pressed against the keyhole, she slams into a wall.

Naia looks up to find herself pressed against the thigh of a giantess whose head is higher than the tops of the stalls. Her belly, the texture of clotted cream, quivers with her laughter. Her joints are indents in tough dough. Even her kneecaps are dimpled. She towers over Naia with her hands on her hips, just a patch of cloth shields her womanhood.

"What are you gaping at?" she booms. "Never seen this much woman before?" She clutches her breasts, her rolls surging.

Naia backs away. She didn't come for the performers, to be reminded by those in costume that she too is in costume, even tonight. Beyond the giantess, a silver-plated busker plants a silver stake in the dirt and lifts his body above it like a lever, freezing horizontal to the ground. Children sidle over to drop coins in the silver bucket beneath him and dash away as he cranks his body back to earth in a mechanical bow.

Naia lingers at a booth where hunched birds of prey shift on their perches, their talons gnashing the wood. She marvels at their barely tamed wildness and presses closer as their handler extends a leather-padded arm. A bird shuffles onto his sleeve with a squint-eyed glare, as if resenting its audience. Avoiding its accusing gaze, Naia moves on, lured by a velvet tent rippling at the edge of the boardwalk. A veiled figure peels back the tent's lips, her bracelets jangling, beckoning Naia inside.

The air is so thick with smoke that Naia is momentarily blinded. Eyes watering, blinking through the haze, she begins to make out the fortune teller reclining in a nest of pillows. Black silk bunches at her breasts. A serpent winds around her waist. She is surrounded by women on their knees in the dirt, knitting the air with their hands. They wear necklaces of crosses and moons and orbs of hair. Be-ringed and bare-headed, the witch burns birds in an ash pit smoking with cigarette butts.

The women turn with bleary eyes, their makeup running down their faces like tracks of oil. One catches her eye, a woman whose face is creased with grief, her eyes haunted, her mouth open as if she has seen a ghost. It's Claire's mother, lost among the women, spelling her daughter into existence. And just as quickly as hope had flared to life in the woman's face, it dies again and she turns back to the smoking fire.

Struggling to breathe, Naia grapples with the curtain folds to reemerge into the crisp sea air. The tent seals shut behind her.

"Pet my pussy?" a little girl asks, and steps aside to reveal a two-headed cat tethered to a silver string.

The child laughs and the cat snarls from both mouths. It swipes at the hem of Naia's dress as she reels away, her breath coming short, the crowd around her dissolves into a dizzying jumble. Lights spark in front of Naia's eyes. She is the only real thing on the boardwalk—and in this moment she even questions her own reality, spinning in a stolen dress, wearing a dead girl like a costume.

Naia concentrates on what she knows to be real: the soggy air, the screaming gulls, the pang of hunger in her gut. She clasps her hands, digging her nails into her palms. Calmed a bit by the pain, she turns and is caught, hypnotized, by a booth where a wisp of cloud dances above a copper funnel. The woman in the booth twirls a paper cone over the funnel until it billows into a pink cloud. Naia exchanges a few dollars for the cone and, following the lead of a small boy sitting on a nearby bench, she touches her tongue to it. The cloud suffuses her mouth with a flavor she had never imagined and can't begin to describe.

She devours it and, drowning her unease in viscous joy, stuffs herself with popcorn from an oily paper box and baklava from a tent with pillows strewn across the ground. She tears into fried dough, dusting her chin with powdered sugar. After a diet of brine, she marvels at the variety of tastes and textures, and the awakening of her innate ability to distinguish them all. She eats until her tongue is numb with lemon ice. Her fingers are sticky and her mouth tastes like spun sugar and grease, and she is still hungry for more. Every bite feeds her hunger.

• • •

Ceto shrinks before her sisters, fighting the impulse to turn her back and shield herself from them. Their horror reveals the cheapness of the knock-off sirenhood she has constructed and plunges her back to the time when her days were dark and unchanging. She had not conceived of sensations more agonizing than hunger. Ceto envies her sisters their blank-eyed indifference, their invulnerable monstrousness. Worse, she fears them.

"What do you have to show for your defiance?" they demand.

"I have built a kingdom," she says, raising her chin.

They turn their blank eyes to the cliffs. Ceto follows their gaze to the empty parking lots, where the banner proclaiming "Live Mermaids" has come untied from one utility pole and whips in the wind. Her sisters shake their heads in unison, shedding bits of bone from their blood-matted hair. Their beauty is all the more striking for their savagery.

"Are you not ashamed of your indolence?" they ask.

Ceto tries to fix them with the glare that had humbled even the most barbarous of men.

"I don't know the meaning of shame," she says.

"We do not believe you." Her sisters curl their fingers around Ceto's wrists, their nails clacking together. "You belong to the sea and she intends to reclaim you. She has revealed to us a way for you to return."

Shock radiates down Ceto's body. She jerks her hands, but they tighten their fingers until her bones grind together.

"I do not want to go back." Her voice wavers with uncertainty. She hadn't entertained regret when returning to the sea seemed impossible. Furious with herself, with her sisters, she tears her hands from their grip. Their talons rend her knuckles.

Her sisters share a gutting laugh.

"Are you not weary of trivial human dramas? Come home, where you have no concern save your next meal."

Ceto cannot recall the abandon with which she'd charted the ocean or the fervor that had led her to saw the scales from her body. She is simply tired now, and still—and always has been—hungry. If she truly could return to the sea, she would need no longer earn a living, or navigate Galene's passions, or worry about her daughter's insubordination, or her mortality. She could return to oblivion. What a relief it would be.

"The sea grants us immortality because we feed her bloodlust," her sisters say. "A gift has ignited her hunger. She thanks you for the girl."

Ceto shudders at the thought of her sisters circling the child like sharks, tearing into her water-logged flesh with their teeth and fingernails. She, too, had scavenged without pity.

"She demands blood again," they say, and release her burning wrists. "To return to us, you must make a sacrifice to the sea."

Ceto's reluctant pity for the girl invokes her love for Naia and its flip-side: the terror that had gripped her when the child tore from her body breathless and bloody. Panic clutches her now as she imagines what might be happening to Naia.

"No." Ceto denies the regret she has come to know all too well. "I made my choice long ago." The emotions she longs to escape are the very ones that bind her here. Ceto turns her back on her sisters for a second time.

• • •

With five dollars left in her purse, Naia wonders what Claire would have bought and scans the stalls for a souvenir befitting the girl whose life she has borrowed. A necklace, maybe, or a magnet. She peruses bins of gemstones and mirrored shelves of fighting fish drifting in plastic cups, slashing their fins at their own reflections. Among a display of painted shells, a pickled baby shark hovers in a jar of vinegar. Its eyes are open. She reels away from it, coming face to face with herself.

The back of the stall is crowded with posters of the sirens. Here is Naia as the Aquatic Infant, her arms outstretched toward Ceto.

Pins and magnets and jewelry and mugs all bear her image. Postcards are printed with her vital stats and answers to questions no one had ever asked her, and all untrue (her favorite color is *not* pink). Her face is on T-shirts, calendars, coasters, soap—even fishnet panties that read, "I can hold my breath all night."

One poster features a recent photograph of Naia glancing over her shoulder mid-turn, her hair billowing around her, her too-tight tail stretched across her backside.

She's always been a performer—but until this moment, she hadn't fully realized she's a commodity. Everywhere she goes, she's Ceto's daughter, ever in the presence of an audience. It was naive to think she could escape sirenhood here; that she could pass as a normal girl when she is reminded at every turn that she is a carnival freak. She is trapped in so many more ways than she had imagined.

Naia backs out of the booth, her eyes blurring with tears. For all that the boardwalk had seemed so distant from Sirenland, it was not far enough to evade her mother's reach. Her body aches to run.

A spotlight flicks on at Naia's feet, casting an illuminated circle before her. Dust motes drift like snowflakes through the light that carves a meditative space into the whirr and rumble of the boardwalk. A man strides onto the makeshift stage. Naked but for ragged jean shorts and a tool belt bearing a hammer and dagger, he carries a leather case and a stool over his shoulder. He places the stool at his feet in the center of the spotlight and sets the case on top. When he opens the lid, the spotlight kindles hundreds of nails and needles skewering a red velvet cushion. Each needle is topped with a bell.

Naia is captivated despite herself; she leans in as the man plucks one from the cushion and pinches his cheek between two fingers to lift skin from bone. He slides the needle through his cheek until its point emerges, forming a steel stitch. A crowd begins to gather, and Naia's pulse riots as if she were the one onstage. She has never been part of an audience before.

The man pierces his eyebrow and, pinch after pinch, works his way across his face, down his neck and shoulders to his torso, moving from needles to nails until he's punctured the whole of his shocked flesh. With the same slow precision, he clears his case from the stool and kneels to press one side of his head against the seat. He sets a nail into his ear canal.

Accompanied by sickened groans of delight from the audience, he brings his hammer down on the nail, punching it smoothly into his ear. He repeats the piercing on the other side, then slides his tongue onto the stool and drives his final nail through it. Robed in steel, he bows with a shiver of bells.

The Pin Man removes the final tool from his belt with reverence. He holds up the dagger by its leather hilt, turning the blade to catch the light, and flings it at the spectators, who recoil in alarm. It falls just short of the crowd, quivering point-down in the boards at Naia's feet.

His gaze pins Naia in place. The crowd turns their expectant faces to her. The Pin Man gestures to the knife.

Without conscious thought, she assumes her stage persona, and tips her head in a mocking bow. But she is uneasy as she pries the knife from the boards. This show is unfamiliar, and she is uneasy straddling the roles of performer and audience. The knife is heavier than she would have expected and the blade gleams in the spotlight. The Pin Man slides the nail out of his tongue.

"What's your name, darlin'?" he shouts, lifting her chin with one twanging finger.

She meets his eyes, imagining a flicker of recognition in them.

"Claire." The dead girl's name rises to her lips like a ghost.

"Well, Claire," he says, lingering over the name, "you'll have the satisfaction of killing me tonight." He places his palm over his heart, where the skin puckers almost imperceptibly.

"If it helps, you can pretend I'm an ex-boyfriend." He winks, chiming the pins in his eyebrow.

"That won't be necessary." Naia positions the knifepoint against his chest. The audience chuckles and she flushes with the pleasure of having made them laugh. She had made audiences laugh often enough, but had never *heard* their laughter through the glass. It is a surprising delight, and yet another experience she'd never realized she was missing out on, another deprivation to add to her growing list.

Although the Pin Man has proven himself a master of trickery, she hesitates, studying the knife for seams that would collapse the blade against his skin or a catch in the hilt that would retract the steel. There is no evidence of deception.

A warning siren wails over the boardwalk, heralding a storm. The Ferris wheel chairs swing in the sky as heavy clouds catch and break around them.

Naia pushes the knife against the Pin Man's chest. His skin yields to the blade like parting sand. The knife scrapes bone, but he holds her eyes with no hint of pain. He smells like sawdust and steel. Nausea rises in her stomach but she resists the impulse to pull away. She tightens her fingers, cursing herself for playing into his ribald showmanship. She knows better than to abdicate control. She is an accomplished performer, and she has committed to this act.

Naia pushes deeper, and the Pin Man wraps his fingers around her hand. She glances up, and he catches her gaze. There are green-gold flecks in the depths of his eyes, reminding Naia of stars. She stares into them as, together, they drive the blade forward until the hilt meets his chest. The Pin Man presses her palm over his heart for the space of a shared breath. She startles at his touch. His skin is hot and his heart pounds against her fingers. Then he swings their joined hands into the air and commands the audience, "Give the girl a round of applause!"

One person claps and, as if awakening from a spell, the rest of the crowd begins to cheer. The Pin Man turns in a circle to prove his impalement to the crowd. They gasp at the sight of the knifepoint protruding from beneath his left shoulder blade. Naia claps as hard as the rest of them, relieved to be part of the audience again. The intimacy of the performance left her breathless and dizzy. It has nothing to do with the man's heat or his chest or his beautiful eyes, she tells herself.

The warning siren wails. The edges of the tents flail and crack, and the vendors rush to strap them down as a curtain of rain swings over the sea.

"Take this out, would you, so I can accept my accolades?" As he wraps Naia's fingers around the hilt, the sky cracks open and rain pummels the boardwalk.

Naia raises her face to the storm. She will not sneak back to Sirenland as if she's committed a crime. She will not slip back into her sleeping mother's arms and pretend to be the perfect siren daughter. She is tired of being meek, tired of mourning forbidden experiences and fearing her own strangeness.

The Pin Man steps back from Naia, and the blade gives way. His body returns it to the air with a sickening swell of skin. He holds her eyes as if he can see the seismic shift that has upended everything inside her.

"Thank you," he says with a wink. "Claire."

8

Ceto clasps the Sailor's Ruin, inviting the rain to whip her back. Her fingernails have carved pits into her palms. Although her sisters have returned to the depths of the sea, the wind plays with the remnants of their terrible laughter as if mocking her.

She had devoured men; now she performs for them. It is necessary, she reminds herself. She must maintain the world she has built to rule, the world she made so Naia will never know the bottomless craving that had driven Ceto to renounce her power. She does it all for Naia—and her daughter is careless with the life Ceto sells out daily to protect. Panic engulfs her, daring her to imagine the worst—and to picture it in horrific detail.

She sees Naia tethered to the ocean floor with a rope sawing through her ankle bones. Naia at knifepoint with tears glittering in her eyes. Naia surrounded by jeering men. Ceto commands herself to stop, but she deserves this torture. The truth is that she doesn't know what Naia could be doing. Galene *does* know the child better than Ceto. Even the daycare providers had realized she was a bad mother. She had been failing Naia from the moment she was born.

Ceto leans into the storm, entreating it to thrash the human emotion from her body. The thought comes unbidden: If she returned to her sisters, she'd need no longer worry about Naia. She'd no longer care about anything.

Beyond the barrier, a fishing boat convulses in the sea. The waves hoist and smash it on the rocks, spewing the wreckage toward the cove. Fishermen grasp at the boat's splintering boards, screaming for help as the breakers tow them under. Ceto's sisters have sent it as a message, or a dare.

The sea tosses a body at the Sailor's Ruin. It's the fishmonger who had saved Naia so many years ago. He's limp in the sea's grasp, his eyes glazed. A clear invitation from her sisters. She will refuse for Naia's sake, if not her own, and prove that she will never return to the sea. She is powerful enough to hold Naia—to hold them all—in the calm eye of Sirenland against the rest of the world.

Embracing the threshing violence, Ceto slips from the rock into the storm-laden waves, allowing them to drag her toward the fishmonger. She loops her arm around his shoulders and he presses his forehead into her breasts as she tows him to safety.

His body paints a red stripe up the sand, but his pulse is still strong beneath her fingers. Ceto is struck, as so often before, by the fragility of human life, when even such a brawny man as this can be brought down by the wind.

She rests beside him on the beach. The alluring scent of his blood, turned acrid with pain, awakens her craving. She'd learned to withstand the urge to hunt, had become skilled at stopping before she takes too much. But she misses the sailors who'd tasted like sun breaking through the waves. She'd once found their unfathomable passions enticing. Now she knows better. Emotions are a burden all humans must bear.

The fishmonger moans in her arms. Her stomach spasms. It has been so long since she had indulged her hunger. Ceto had long ago learned moderation; she knows how to take just enough to satisfy the craving. She will allow herself just a taste, a reward for her restraint.

Throbbing with hunger, Ceto dips her tongue into the wound at the base of his neck. The boldness of his blood reminds her of her husband's morning coffee, black, no sugar, and prickles the back of her throat. His life pulses between her teeth.

A wordless cry sails across the beach and Ceto turns toward her daughter's voice. The savage ache of relief brings her back to herself. She wipes the back of her hand across her mouth.

Naia skims across the beach, her legs bare, her rain-soaked dress clinging to her thighs and belly and breasts. She stops a yard away, taking in the scene. The fishmonger groans.

Where have you been? Ceto wants to demand, to rail against her, but she holds her tongue, registering the wariness in her daughter's eyes.

"Come," she says, and reaches for Naia.

Her daughter's legs wobble as if she longs to run, but she allows Ceto to guide her down to the sand.

"Press here." She holds Naia's palm to the man's neck.

Naia doesn't flinch. She clamps her hand against the wound, the tendons straining in her slender arms, and turns to her mother for further instruction.

Ceto is struck by the familiarity of her expression. Her eyebrows are lifted, her lips tight. This is how Naia used to look at her when asking endless questions about her father and aunts, her mother and strangers and the boardwalk and the world beyond it. Unsatisfied with Ceto's answers, she'd stopped asking questions many years ago. Naia rarely speaks to her now.

Confusion tugs at the corners of Naia's mouth as she studies the blood seeping through her fingers. She breathes deep, bracing herself.

"What does he taste like?" she whispers haltingly, as if she knows she's crossing a line from which there's no return.

Ceto's breath catches. The fishmonger's blood burns her throat.

"What do you mean?" Ceto manages to sound impassive, as if Naia had simply asked about the weather, but her chest is tight with the effort of feigning calm.

"I saw you," Naia says, adopting the imperious tone her mother uses with Sirenland's vendors. "And I'm not a child. I know you've done it to all of us, and I want to know why." Her voice wavers with tension, but in an attempt at flippancy, she adds, "You're already angry at me, so I may as well ask."

Coast Guard sirens join the storm warning that rings out across the ocean. Naia stares at her hands pressed to the fishmonger's wound. She bends over him as if over the edge of a cliff, preparing to jump, and he opens his eyes, arching against the sand in pain.

Ceto holds her breath. When her daughter had transfixed that boy on the beach, she'd known they would have to reckon with her hunger—but she'd hoped to have more time. She hadn't decided how much to tell Naia about her origins, and now it seemed the decision might be made for her. She finds herself urging her daughter to *go on, learn who you are.*

The Coast Guard helicopter careens over the waves, illuminating the wreckage. Light streams over Naia. Men in red vests invade the beach with stretchers, the storm thrashing around them, and Ceto slithers into the sea. She cannot be seen here in her tail with blood on her lips. She knows what men do to monsters.

Naia scrambles to her feet, calling out for help, but the wind snatches her voice away. Her hands drip with blood. Ceto's heart aches with compassion for her daughter, and contempt for herself. She is the vilest of monsters: a bad mother.

• • •

Ceto disrobes alone. The shortcomings of this body are all the more egregious in contrast to her sisters' monstrous youth. When she'd shorn her tail, she hadn't considered the limitations she would inherit along with humanity, so eager had she been to experience their rich inner world. How unfair that depth of feeling is attended by mortality, but humans feel too much and touch too hard to last.

Witnessing her body dying little by little is a slow torture made all the more unbearable by the girls who flaunt their youth before her on the beach. A deep pain is gathering at her temples. A knock on the door sharpens it. Only Galene is allowed entrance into this room, and she hasn't come to Ceto since the girl's death.

She waits. When an uncomfortable silence has built on the opposite side of the door, she commands, "Enter," and watches in the mirror as Nixie slinks into the room. Ceto does not turn around.

"I'm sorry," Nixie says. "I wouldn't have come if it wasn't important."

Standing just inside the doorway in her dressing gown with her eyes downcast, she seems younger now than when she'd first arrived as Shelley from Kansas City. She'd brought her own tail and proclaimed she'd made it herself, demonstrating how the scales shimmered as they caught the light. She'd practiced Ceto's moves at the YMCA, she said, and could already hold her breath for two minutes. She sweated earnestness in spicy waves.

"How old are you?" Ceto had asked.

"Twenty-one." Shelley tipped up her chin in defiance, revealing her wildly beating jugular. She couldn't have been older than seventeen.

"I will not turn away any woman with a true need for Sirenland," Ceto said. "But I cannot risk the scandal of an angry mother dragging her home."

Shelley set her jaw, like Naia at her most petulant.

"My mother won't care," she said. "Believe me."

Shelley's blood had been laced with bitterness, along with sugary enthusiasm and clove-tinged need. Nixie still sweats desperation; it ripples off her, making her a favorite of the sailors.

"I'm worried about Naia," she says. "I saw her heading for the boardwalk—*wearing a dress*. I thought you'd want to know, because of what happened to that girl?" Her voice lifts at the end like a kite snapping free of its string.

Ceto fixes her with a mast-splitting glare.

"Why are *you* out of bed?" she demands, daring Nixie to question her judgment, her fitness as a mother, her authority.

Nixie flinches as if struck.

"I was in the lavatory and saw her from the window." Nixie clasps her hands below her breasts. "I hope you won't punish her *too* severely."

The catlike satisfaction in her eyes betrays her true reason for informing on Naia. She's always been jealous. Ceto knows she's like a mother to Nixie, but she doesn't know how to give her what she seems to crave. She's barely a mother to Naia.

"This is none of your concern." She dismisses Nixie with a flick of her wrist. "Return to your room."

"It's just—"

Nixie closes her eyes, as if gathering herself. Ceto raises an eyebrow. Nixie has never disobeyed a direct command.

"She's been so sheltered—she doesn't know how people are, how men can be." Worry shivers in her voice, taking Ceto by surprise. "Don't you think, maybe, someone should go after her?"

Ceto drags her nails along the arms of her throne. Perhaps she has misjudged Nixie. She too masks weakness with savagery. It's possible she even loves Naia. But doubt is a disease, and it is spreading among her sirens.

"Naia must make her own mistakes," Ceto says.

Nixie clutches the doorframe, fortifying herself to meet Ceto's eyes.

"When I finally told my mom that my stepdad was . . . hurting me—" her mouth stiffens as if the words are shards of glass—"she didn't believe me. Or maybe she did, which is worse, because she didn't *do* anything. My mother didn't save me."

She squeezes her eyes shut, but tears leak down her face.

This is the most Nixie has ever shared about her life, beyond what Ceto could gather from the hurt simmering in her blood. She is taken aback by her impulse to gather Nixie in her arms and comfort her as her own mother never had. But she is not Nixie's mother. Her sirens' past lives are irrelevant. And Nixie's doubt is dangerous.

"Trust that I will handle it, as I handle any siren who disobeys the laws of Sirenland." Ceto shades her voice with studied ruthlessness. Nixie grinds the tears from her eyes with her knuckles, as if punishing her body for its betrayal.

"Would you care to challenge more of my decisions? That is the only reason I can imagine you would still be standing before me." Nixie jerks away as if struck. "Do you have suggestions for the bar menu, perhaps, or how I should dress my hair?" Nixie shakes her head, scattering tears as she backs toward the door. "Come now, you have such strong opinions—best spit them out before they choke you."

Ceto frowns at her reflection as the door shuts behind her. That had been harsh, but necessary, because Nixie is right.

She *should* speak with her daughter about the boardwalk, and what she saw, and nearly did, upon returning to the cove. She should punish Naia—Ceto has certainly never withheld punishment—but her own sisters' discipline had only hastened Ceto toward her fate.

9

There was once a wretched fisherman whose corner of the ocean had run dry. Nixie emerges from the conch shell in black leggings and a fishing vest, wielding a fishing rod and net. She settles cross-legged on the lip of the black hole and sends her line into its depths.

He had caught nothing for three days and was becoming ever weaker and more desperate. On the third day, he implored the sea to reward his patience, offering in return the lives of the children he might someday sire.

Nixie's pole jerks in her grasp, and she struggles to tame the jolting line. Straining against the mysterious weight, she draws Halia over the edge of the hole, hooked through the cheek.

Although the siren claws at the fisherman, he clasps her to his chest. Their battle becomes a dance of wills. Tethered by his hand, she spins out and back into the circle of his arms.

As the siren abandons herself to the dance, her desperate writhing transforms into a different kind of passion. She begins to follow his lead. When she throws her head back in wanton surrender, the fisherman rips off her tail.

Yards of white tulle unfurl, billowing around her legs. The fisherman stuffs her tail into a leather sack and pulls the siren into an embrace, sealing their bodies together.

From beneath her gown, the siren births a catfish. A second, and still a third slip from between her legs and glide away as she buries her face in her hands, mourning the children the sea has stolen from her. The fisherman tries to hold her, to partake of her grief, but it is too vast to be contained.

The siren finds strength in anguish. She breaks free of the fisherman and, stealing a final glance at him, plunges into the black hole where he cannot follow. The fisherman retreats to the surface in despair as the first strains of the Siren's Song swell at half-tempo, ghost-like in their distortion.

We are not your average women / We are sirens of the deep . . . Three giant catfish emerge from the hole, their silicone hides gleaming and whiskers quivering in the current. The costume fits snugly over Naia's head and extends past her torso, pinning her arms to her sides. Although she admires its craftsmanship, the costume squeezes her ribs and the eyeholes concealed beneath the jaw add a layer of difficulty to her performance. Naia and her catfish sisters weave around each other in a complex dance, graceful despite their bulk.

The youngest catfish longs to know the father who abandoned

her and ventures again and again to the seam between sea and sky, awaiting a glimpse of him.

Naia squints at the spectators beyond the glass, seeking to divine their faces as they follow the sweep of her hips. Even as an ugly fish, she effortlessly manipulates their gaze.

What would her aunts say if they knew the temptation to which she had nearly succumbed? Although she had not drunk from the fishmonger's throat, she cannot rid her mouth of his phantom blood. When she'd asked her mother about its taste, Naia had caught the flinch in her eyes and understood she had given voice to the unspeakable. And that was after running off to the boardwalk, in a dress.

Ceto must be beyond enraged. The only reason Naia can imagine her mother hasn't punished her yet is that she's devising a punishment suitable for such radical transgressions. Her fingers quiver, and Naia tamps down her anxiety. The boardwalk had been worth whatever punishment her mother will mete out. Her senses are inundated by the caress of Claire's skirt against her legs, the heat of the Pin Man's fingers on her knuckles, the feel of his blade in her fist. As awful as it is to await retribution, the idea of never again experiencing such simple human pleasures is far worse.

The catfish's sisters follow her, imploring her to be content with the sisterhood that gives meaning to their brief lives. They tell her that no good can come of longing. They thrash and berate her, but punishment only pushes her farther from them, until she lives more at the surface than in the sea.

Her sisters come to her a final time, pleading for her to return with them, but she denies them yet again. As Galene, the eldest catfish, turns away in grief, she slams face-first into the observation window. Stunned, she flips belly-up.

There is the pause of an in-held breath.

And then, the audience laughs.

Naia's vision blurs with rage. The audience laughs at her aunt as she struggles to right herself—laughs at all of them. For the first time when performing, she feels stupid.

Nixie speeds the show along, returning to the black hole to cast the fisherman's line. Naia takes hold. Striving to imbue the scene with gravity, she blinks the catfish's eyes open and closed mournfully, but it's no use. Galene bumps into Naia and the costume slides up, revealing her bare midriff. The show is now a comedy.

Ceto will be furious. Sirens can be sexy and flirtatious and dangerous—even kitschy—but they cannot be silly.

Naia holds to the script, tries to tell the fisherman that she is his daughter, but she did not inherit her mother's magical ability to speak. The catfish's mouth opens and closes impotently. When the fisherman, believing her to be no more than a fish, scoops her into his net, the audience roars with laughter.

The curtains close at last. Halia tugs the catfish over Maris's head and they surge into one another's arms, relieved as always to reclaim their twin at the end of a performance. They break apart to free Naia and Galene from their costumes and together, swan dive toward the black hole and spread their arms to clasp one another's hands. Galene fumbles for Naia's fingers and squeezes them in apology.

The sirens bow their heads above the hole in deference to the source of their spring, but Naia cannot tame her restless gaze tonight. The lines at the corners of Galene's mouth are as deeply carved as marionette joints. Nixie grasps Ceto's hand like a child. Ceto is as enigmatic as ever.

As the sirens flow up to the tube, Naia follows Galene to the edge of the tank where the seagrass obscures the entrance to the private show. She reaches out to stall Galene, who turns to her with stricken eyes, clutching her costume to her chest. Naia pushes her gently toward the tube.

She hadn't planned to take Galene's place for the private show, but it feels right. She'll spare her aunt from further humiliation—and finally learn what happens in the strange, mirrored cavern. There must be a reason she's never performed the private show like her mother and aunts. She is tired of secrets. Naia brushes off her aunt's pleading embrace and darts through the grass. It seals behind her.

She pushes into the entrance of the shallow cave. The sea is colder in this dark crevice, making her skin prickle and her nipples rise. Music thrums through the water, a pounding bass different than the songs of the sirens' performances. Naia waits in the expectant darkness, her heart throbbing in her throat.

The glass before Naia reflects her wide eyes back to her. Galene still thinks of her as a child, as does the audience who'd laughed at her, as does everyone who sees the posters on the boardwalk. She stares into the glass, seeing herself as Claire had, a girl in a fake tail. The Pin Man had seen her differently, as a girl in a crowd worthy of his attention.

A light turns on beyond the glass and Naia's reflection gives way to a booth large enough only for a single patron. A man sits there, pressed close to the window. The music shifts into a languid pulse, prompting movements different from any Naia has performed. It undulates, stroking her sides like a dance partner. Her muscles twitch, primed by thousands of performances to respond to the mere suggestion of a beat, but Naia is pinned by the man's eyes. They are sad and desperate, and do not reach her face. She shrinks away from the want in them. His hand moves in his lap.

Naia's stomach clenches, as when Claire's brother had whispered his hot breath into her ear, assailing her with his hunger. Now, as before, she's trapped by the constraints of her performance. She has put herself before this man, offered herself up for his entertainment. Her aunts had suggested that private shows were empowering; Galene with her whip, Nixie with her unbound hair. This can't be right. Or else, there's something wrong with *her* for finding this vile. Once again, she lacks the experience to know how she should feel.

Naia backs against the wall and wraps her arms around her

belly. The man leans closer. His mouth is slack, his eyes unfocused. It doesn't matter what she does, or doesn't do, she realizes sickly. He will take his pleasure in her no matter what. She may as well be a photograph or a doll. She wants to cry. She wants to rip him apart. Instead, she closes her eyes and waits in the darkness behind her eyelids.

Naia's ribs ache with need, but she holds herself still until the pressure in her chest becomes unbearable. She forces her eyes open. The glass is dark again. She pushes through the sea grass and gulps from the oxygen hose. Her diaphragm fills, releasing the clamp of her ribs. She is not alone in the tank.

Two bodies, pale in their nakedness, twine together above the black hole, tethered by the oxygen hoses snaking down to the rocks. The man is coated with dark fur and his body is broad and hard. He envelopes the woman's smaller frame, bending her against his chest with his gleaming hook. Nixie's distinctive hair billows around them. The bartender sips from the hose, seemingly no stranger to this routine.

The rock scrapes Naia's shoulders. She's heard her aunts talk about this primal act, but she had never been able to imagine it. Even as she edges up toward the tube, she cannot tear her gaze from the bodies writhing below her. She burns with shame and a deep, agonizing need.

Although at first Nixie seemed overpowered by the bartender's thick limbs, she wraps her legs around his waist and digs her heels into his back, riding him with the current. The bartender buries his face in her neck. He clutches her hair in his fist and yanks her head back. Nixie's eyes glitter with triumph—and cut to Naia across the bartender's cheek.

Naia knows she should look away, but she holds her aunt's startled, exultant gaze. She will not flee from Nixie, from this, like a child. She will stop being oblivious.

Naia summons the feeling of the freckled boy's hands tangled in her hair and the taste of his fear, her disgust as the man beyond the glass took his pleasure in her, her excitement when the Pin Man singled her out of a crowd. Each had claimed power over her, each different in ways she cannot yet explain. But along with those uneasy sensations, she'd also sensed the stirrings of influence over those men, and it felt better to dominate rather than to be dominated as she had been all her life. It felt *good*. She does not yet understand power, but she will learn to wield it.

10

Naia strides to the boardwalk in full view of Sirenland. She has already broken so many rules; let Ceto add this offense to the record. Surely, whatever punishment her mother is devising couldn't get any more extreme. There's no reason to hide.

Naia wants to hold the knife again. She wants to plunge the blade into the Pin Man's chest and pull it gleaming from his breast bone, evidence of her mastery over him. She wants to make him bleed this time.

The cove below is deserted but for a solitary figure trudging along the sand. Claire's brother and father have returned home. Her mother remains, haunting the beach.

As before, the boardwalk bustles with tourists and vendors and performers. As before, the veiled woman peels back the tent's velvet lips, her bracelets jangling. Naia pushes past her, ignoring the girl who invites her again to stroke the two-headed cat. She skirts the giantess leaning against the roof of an ice cream stall, smoking a cigar. She is not tempted by the glittering array of gems or the fighting fish or fried foods. She doesn't stop until she reaches the Pin Man's makeshift stage.

He's not there. There is no spotlight. Bare feet and sandals pass over the boards where knife etchings are the only evidence of his existence.

Naia worries at the hem of her crumpled dress. It's oily in this heat. The fabric chafes under her arms and an algal scent blooms from the pits of the sleeves. The fishmonger's blood streaks the skirt.

She waits. The families leave the boardwalk, replaced by rowdy teens. She waits, watching the Ferris wheel scoop up and discharge riders, until the ride has shed itself five times over. And she waits until at last, the spotlight finds the boards at her feet.

A crowd gathers around her, drawn to the light. As before, the Pin Man strides onto the makeshift stage naked but for his jean shorts and tool belt. The spectators murmur among themselves with confused anticipation, and Naia grins. She knows what's coming, and they do not.

As before, the first half of his performance is stark and almost reverent. The Pin Man ignores the audience, sliding pin after pin into his flesh. His eyes are glazed with purpose, and Naia studies him at her leisure. Unlike the bartender, his skin is hairless and gleams as if oiled. He is all sinew and bone, tendon and muscle.

She does not want to find him appealing—she never again wants to find a man appealing—but as she sweeps her gaze down his naked chest, she can't help the twist in her stomach, or her desire for him to notice her, to remember her. It's not the same flutter of anticipation she'd felt with the freckled boy. This is a more intense desire born from the knowledge that she has influence, even if she doesn't yet know what to do with it.

He hammers nails into his ears and tongue. Then, robed in steel, he acknowledges the spectators at last, setting off the bells as he bows.

The Pin Man flashes the knife from his belt. Again, he raises the blade to the light and Naia's breath catches in anticipation. She steps forward. His eyes alight on her and flit away, and he hurls the knife point-down at the feet of another girl in the crowd. She squeals and hides her flushed cheeks in her hands. Naia is surprised by the anger that leaps hot and sudden in her chest at his rejection.

"What's your name, darlin'?" he booms, lifting the girl's chin with one twanging finger.

Naia shrinks in humiliation as he carries out the same act, down to the wink and his pin-cloaked hand wrapped around the girl's fingers on the knife hilt.

Naia had been foolish to think he would remember her. She should be relieved that his performance had not been as intimate as he had suggested last night, but she is mortified by his indifference. She'd thought she'd felt a kinship with him, that he'd singled her out for a reason, but she'd been nothing more to him than she'd been to the man in the black box—a prop in service to a fantasy. A hand to hold his knife.

The Pin Man encourages the girl to thrust the blade into his chest, but she shakes her head with a nervous giggle. He whispers into her ear. She closes her eyes, her fingers loose around the hilt, and he pushes forward, driving the knife into his chest. The girl screeches in disgusted delight. Naia hates her for her feigned helplessness and the Pin Man for accommodating it.

When he scans the audience and his eyes brush hers again, Naia catches them and grabs hold, inviting the magnetism that had lured the boy into deeper water. The thrilling, aching connection unspools between them. This is what she came for. She owns it this time.

Naia holds the Pin Man in the spotlight, his bells tinkling. The power she wields over him jumps in her stomach. The audience cheers, but the Pin Man stands in the circle with his arms at his sides, his pupils swollen. The crowd begins to shuffle in confusion, their applause waning. As the crowd trickles away, Naia keeps him pinned, savoring the current that runs between them, heating her skin.

She draws the Pin Man to the circle's edge, his eyes clouded with need. She wraps her fingers around the knife handle and gives it a brutal twist in his chest. *That* is for her mortification. He does not even flinch.

Naia tugs the blade from his body to test it against her palm. It bites into her flesh and she drops it at his feet, snapping the link between them. The rush of power she'd experienced when in control of him, and his knife, drains away, leaving her nervous as his eyes clear.

"Hi, Claire," he says, scooping the knife off the boards.

"You remember me." She resents him for the spark of excitement he ignites in her chest.

"I never forget a girl who's pierced my heart," he says, in his jovial performer's voice, but the confusion tugging at his eyes reminds Naia of the boy who had stared dumbly after her on the beach. He slings his stool over his shoulder and picks up his leather case. They stare at each other across the dirt.

Naia hadn't thought this far ahead. She lifts one bare foot to scratch her shin with dirty toes. The scent of bug spray wafts up the neck of her dress.

"Hungry?" He tosses the question at her.

She nods. She is always hungry.

"Be right back." He steps over the cat who guards the fortune teller's tent and ducks through the velvet folds.

Had he asked her to eat with him, or was he simply inquiring if she was hungry? When she'd left Sirenland tonight, she hadn't imagined what she'd do beyond the edge of the Pin Man's stage. Naia is taken aback by a rush of shame. She has inflicted on the Pin Man the same injustice spectators have exacted on *her* daily since she was the Aquatic Infant: she hadn't thought of him as a person apart from his performance. The idea of engaging with the man behind the pins makes her want to run—but she's curious. The cat's four eyes follow her as she presses close to the slit between the curtains.

"Hey, Wanda," the Pin Man says. When he isn't projecting for an audience, his voice is a few octaves higher. He's younger than he'd seemed onstage.

"Hi, honey." Wanda has the gravelly tone of a heavy smoker. "Good turnout tonight."

Naia squints into the gloom of the tent as the Pin Man sets his case on Wanda's table and pulls the pins from his body with sure movements. He wipes them with rubbing alcohol and sticks them into the velvet cushion. The ritual only takes a few minutes. He scrubs his skin with an alcohol-soaked rag and pulls on a button-up shirt.

"Grabbing a bite," he says. "Mind if I leave my stuff for a while?"

"Sure thing." Wanda leans back on her pillows and closes her eyes. "But be careful with that one. She'll eat you alive."

The cat raises one head to watch as Naia slips away from the curtain, puzzling over the fortune teller's warning. It means nothing, she tells herself; after all, the woman couldn't even find Claire.

"Penny for your thoughts," the Pin Man says as he emerges from the tent, and pulls a coin from her ear.

The boardwalk lights dance in and out of the pockmarks that speckle his eyebrows, the bridge of his nose, his jawline, every exposed inch of skin. The only other evidence of his trade is a nail through one earlobe.

As Naia studies him, he flushes and lifts one side of his lips, as if afraid to fully commit to an expression.

"Sorry, that was stupid," he says, and offers Naia his arm. Startled by its steeliness and his astringent smell, she allows him to lead her through the crowd.

He comes unmoored beyond the spotlight. His joints loosen and he walks as if propelled by an invisible wind at his back. Naia is attracted to his lightness, wishing her body could move as naturally through the air as through the sea.

He guides her past the popcorn and chowder and ice cream to a cart at the end of the boardwalk where he loads his arms with hot dogs and lemonade and gestures with his chin to the Ferris wheel. The kid working the controls ushers them to the head of the line with a suggestive eyebrow waggle.

An empty booth sways before them. The vinyl squeals beneath Naia's thighs as she slides onto the seat, and she brushes her feet in circles, making patterns in the sand strewn across the metal floor. The faint hairs on her arms glint red and then purple when the blue light hits it. The gate slams shut, sealing them together. The bones of her knee rub against the Pin Man's. While her impulse is to shy away from him, she is bewildered by a warring desire to press closer.

Their seat lurches and Naia grips the bar as they rise until there is nothing beneath them but sky, and the boardwalk far below, and the beach beyond, and the dark ocean beyond that, swelling and falling like an animal breathing.

The Pin Man hands her a hot dog with a flourish.

"So, Claire, where ya from?" he asks, with affected nonchalance.

She takes a bite, trying to recall the details of Claire's life.

"New Jersey," she says around a mouthful of food.

"I have family in Jersey." He eats quickly and wipes his lips with a napkin.

"Is that where you're from?"

"No."

She waits, but he stares off into the distance with a deep crease between his brows. Their chair sways suspended. Naia fights the sudden compulsion to jump. She finishes the hotdog instead.

Without looking at her, he asks carefully, "You're what, fifteen?"

"Seventeen."

He nods, complicit in the lie.

"Where do you live when you're not doing this?" she asks, willing him to see her as his equal, to see that she recognizes the man behind the fantasy.

"Haven't decided yet." He speaks haltingly, as if he's moved off the page and is forced to come up with new lines. He turns his full attention to her, claiming her eyes as he had when handing her the knife hilt. "I'd rather hear about you."

No one's ever wanted to know her before—or, they haven't had the opportunity. And she'd always had a script: *I fear I do not understand your request. I was born here. There is no other world than this.* She can't think of anything to say about herself. There's nothing *to* say; she doesn't know if there's even a real Naia beyond who her mother has told her she should be.

"What do you want to know?" she asks.

"We've covered where you're from, so how about: What are your deepest hopes and dreams?" He props his chin on his fist and quirks an eyebrow.

This is so different from conversations among her aunts. With them, there is rarely silence. They talk over each other and dip in and out of a maze Naia often can't follow and rarely tries to. She is content to let their voices wash over her, comforting in their familiarity. With the Pin Man she's perched at a cliff edge of conversation.

"My hopes and dreams . . ."

Does she have hopes and dreams? Not any she can put into words. She has vague and intense longings. She doesn't even know who she is, much less what she wants—except, maybe, to learn who she could be. But that is too vast an answer to his playful question, and he wouldn't understand. Frustration tightens her chest. She should be able to answer basic questions.

The Pin Man bumps her shoulder with his own.

"Lost you again," he says. "How about: Got any brothers or sisters?"

"A brother." Naia recalls the boy's greasy breath in her ear. "He's a jerk."

"A typical guy, then."

This, she can answer, nodding in relief. Her aunts had told her plenty about typical guys.

"What do you like to do?" he asks. Then, as if noting she's at a loss for an answer, adds: "Let me guess: Horseback riding. All girls like horses."

Riding horses! She can't imagine how that would even be possible, but it sounds thrilling and dangerous and strange. Yes, Claire would like riding horses.

"Horses," she affirms. "And bicycles."

What else would Claire do—what else *could* Claire have done, with all the freedom afforded her; all the experiences her aunts had taken for granted and the guests hint at but never explain to her satisfaction.

"Dancing, too. And movies and sunbathing and the SATs." She dredges up Claire's ghost, stitching her together with book characters and details from her aunts' lives and snippets she'd collected from guests. She forgets about the Pin Man in her enthusiasm for creating Claire, painting over a childhood spent performing, inventing friends and vacations and a mother with whom she shares her secrets. Her favorite food is meatloaf and she had her first kiss with a freckled boy in a dark, quiet bus, and he'd been shaking so hard their braces scraped.

"Lucky guy," the Pin Man says, reminding her that he exists. He leans one elbow on the bar, staring at Naia.

She's almost jealous of Claire for holding this man's attention with her simple human life. She likes how he asks her more questions, as if helping her coax Claire into being. Naia likes the version of herself he reflects back to her.

She's been talking so long her throat is dry. It occurs to Naia that the audience has never heard her voice. How impersonal, to watch someone night after night and never once hear them speak. Silence descends between them. She waits, unsure of how to fix it.

"I like talking to you," the Pin Man says, picking up the thread of the conversation as easily as plucking a pin from its cushion. "Most girls just ask if the nails hurt and try to get me to reveal my secrets."

She'd assumed he employed the same kind of trickery as the siren shows, playing on the audience's expectations, building fantasy around a seed of truth. Every performer is entitled to their secrets; Naia would no more expect him to divulge how he pierces his skin without pain than she would reveal how she can breathe underwater for the length of a performance—even if she knew.

But Claire would ask.

"How *do* you do it?"

"You don't really want to know," he says.

"Shouldn't I?"

His lips quirk at one corner. She wonders what it would take to surprise him into a full smile.

"What do you *really* want to know?" he asks.

She sips her lemonade, considering. She's seen the artifice behind every kind of magic. She wants to know about everyday things: how to order breakfast at a restaurant, how to keep your feet from getting wet in the rain, what it feels like to fly in an airplane.

"Where else have you been?"

"All over. I've been everywhere; done everything!" He adopts his showman's bluster, lifting his face to the wind. "I've wrestled alligators and walked across fire and lain on a bed of nails. I've slept under the stars and begged for my breakfast."

"What did you eat?" she asks.

He looks at her, puzzled, and she wonders she's asked an inappropriate question. And then, as if surprising even himself, he breaks into a loud laugh. Naia can't remember the last time she heard such a laugh, and she immediately wants to hear it again. But she doesn't know what she said that was funny.

"Most girls ask about the alligators. No one's ever asked me what I ate for breakfast," he says, trying and failing to recapture his air of nonchalance. "My usual is scrambled eggs, bacon, toast, no butter, coffee, black."

"What other colors does it come in?"

"I'm lactose intolerant," he says, as if that answered the question.

She likes how he waits for her questions and answers them without judgment.

"Tell me about your friends," she demands, recalling the girl she'd brought to her room to try on her tail. The girl whose birthday party she'd attempted to join. Another who'd invited Naia to her family picnic. She'd spent more days than she could count atoning for her transgressions in the lobster cage.

"Wanda's all right," he says.

She waits, but he doesn't elaborate.

"Your family?" she asks.

Something shuts down in his eyes.

"So, Claire!" He pulls his performer persona around himself and holds out his fist like a microphone. "What do you want to do with your life?"

Naia opens her mouth. What had Claire wanted to do with her life? There is more to want than Naia knows exists for her to want. Her desires are a mystery even to herself. Above all, she wants to know what there is to want. The Pin Man lowers his fist.

When the chair slows to a stop, he opens the gate and takes her hand to help her step out. He keeps hold of her, even when they move away from the Ferris wheel to the edge of the thinning crowd. She's never held anyone's hand before, other than her mother's and aunts' during performances. His touch is different. The roughness of his skin is different, and his short, clean fingernails. He's not leading her or keeping her in place. It seems he's holding her hand just to hold her hand.

The casual touch sends tingles up and down Naia's arm, and she recalls Nixie's curves molded to the bartender's hard body. If this simple contact is almost unbearable, she wonders what his touch would feel like against the full length of her skin. The thought fills her with heat and she's suddenly short of breath, aching to run and to press closer to the Pin Man at the same time.

He looks down at her. As if rushing to get the words out before he can stop himself, he asks, "Can I see you again?"

The two-headed cat pads by. As the silence stretches out between them, the Pin Man drops Naia's hand to pick up the cat, pretending to be absorbed in scratching behind its ears. The cat nestles into his arms and fixes its eyes on Naia. Each one is a different color.

Her stomach roils with sugar and fear and pleasure and need. She wants to see him again. She *needs* to be Claire again. In pretending to be like everyone else, she has begun to peel away her siren self and discover who she is beyond the stage.

"I think I can get away tomorrow night, after my mother falls asleep," she says, envisioning a woman in a long nightgown, a glass of sherry on the nightstand, a seedy hotel off the highway. "Meet me at Sirenland."

11

When Naia wades into the bedroom, her mother is asleep with her knees pulled up against her chest, her tail flopped behind her. It's dark beyond the window, quiet but for the thrashing of the sea. Still burning from the Pin Man's touch, Naia can't bear to fold herself into her mother's moist embrace. She holds her breath, sliding past Ceto with barely a ripple, and slips out into the hallway she's only ever seen when carried in her throne. She's already committed so many sins against Sirenland; what's one more?

She turns down a side tunnel she has never had an opportunity to explore, mapping the kingdom's inner sanctum to its public-facing rooms. The fluorescent lights along the ceiling flicker, casting her shadow across the concrete floor.

The tunnel wraps to the left and ends with a door. She presses her cheek against it and, hearing nothing, opens it an industrial kitchen with gleaming steel counters, and a towering refrigerator, which she opens to a blast of cold that shocks her naked skin.

The shelves are stocked with foil-topped platters and plastic containers and bags of sauces and chips and cheese. Naia lifts the lid from a bowl and sniffs the contents. Scallops. She pops one into her mouth and chews its rubbery sweetness while peeking under the foil obscuring other dishes. She finds a mountain of chicken wings, bacon stiffened in its own grease, beer and lemonade and sodas. She dips her finger into a bowl of pale-yellow liquid and sucks off the juice, squeezing her eyes shut against its sharp zest.

The kitchen has been here all this time, and Naia had never thought to look for it. She plucks out a chicken wing and digs the meat from the bones. It's at once crispy and tender, and she swipes the sauce from the corner of her mouth with her tongue, savoring a burst of heat. She guzzles something fizzy that dribbles down her chin and onto her bare breast where it gleams like a pearl at the tip of her nipple.

The door opens. She drops to the ground like a cornered animal. Nixie is frozen in the doorway, her lips parted, her dressing gown brushing the tops of her bare feet. Naia offers her a sheepish smile, and her aunt quickly rearranges her face into a familiar expression of scorn.

"What are you doing?" she demands.

"I was hungry."

Nixie glowers at her, as if waiting for Naia to ask what *she* is doing here, until the open refrigerator begins chiming for attention. Nixie rolls her eyes and holds out a hand. She tugs Naia to her feet.

"I'm hungry, too. Your mother starved me for three days," Nixie says, and adds: "Not that I didn't deserve it."

She reaches into the refrigerator, pushing aside the containers Naia has plundered. As she stretches to the top shelf, she takes a deep breath and says with careful nonchalance, "What you saw in the tank—"

"I didn't see anything," Naia says, her skin blazing.

Nixie glances over her shoulder. A grin tugs at her lips. She kills it before it spreads.

"Okay then." She thrusts a carton of eggs into Naia's hands and dips back into the refrigerator for milk, a plate of butter, a bag of cheese. With the ingredients spread out on the counter, she swipes an apron from a drawer and loops it over Naia's head, then turns her to knot the ties behind her back. Her touch is efficient, but surprisingly gentle.

Nixie grabs a cutting board and an onion from the basket of vegetables next to the stove. Naia's eyes sting as the knife flashes through the onion's translucent flesh.

"Make yourself useful and crack the eggs." Nixie says, as tears trickle down her cheeks from the onions. She slides a pan onto the oven and adds a pat of butter.

Naia plucks an egg from the carton and turns it over in her hand, studying its fragile shell.

"I don't know how," she says.

Nixie covers her hand with her own and raps the egg on the rim of a bowl. She expertly parts the shell and the yolk slides out.

"You do the rest," she says.

By the time Naia has cracked five more eggs into the bowl, yolk dribbles down her hands. She lifts her fingers to her mouth. Nixie catches her wrist.

"Don't," she says. "Salmonella." She dumps the chopped onion into the pan where it sizzles and browns.

"What's that?"

"Doesn't matter. Wash your hands."

She obeys as Nixie pours cream into the eggs and thrashes them until they foam, then folds in a handful of cheese. Naia opens all the cupboards until she finds a stack of clean white plates and carries two to the stove. Nixie pours the eggs into the pan. They watch as the mixture begin to bubble.

Nixie slides a metal scraper under the eggs and flips them over until they're golden, then scoops a portion onto each plate.

"Go on," she says, handing one to Naia, almost shyly.

Naia lifts a forkful, winding strings of melted cheese around the tines.

"So good," she moans through a mouthful of sweet buttery onions and salty cheese and crispy-edged eggs.

Nixie actually laughs.

"It's the one thing I know how to cook," she says. "I made it for my brother a lot."

"Do you miss him?" Naia almost asks, but doesn't, for fear of rupturing this tender spell.

As she leans beside Nixie at the counter in companionable silence, a memory rises to the surface of another time Nixie betrayed tenderness beneath her brittle exterior. When Naia was twelve, she had stripped off her tail in the washroom to find it streaked with blood. In a blind panic, she had scrubbed her thighs until they were raw. Nixie had grown impatient of waiting for the washroom and pushed through the door, where Naia was crouched sobbing on the floor. She had fetched a towel and gently cleaned Naia's legs while she explained their monthly courses. She'd lent Naia another tail for the evening's performance and they'd never spoken of it again.

"So," Nixie asked, with obvious nonchalance. "Do you want to tell me where you were tonight?"

Naia meets her aunt's expectant gaze. It holds no malice, only curiosity and, Naia is surprised to notice, concern. She feels almost close enough to Nixie to tell her about the Pin Man and how his hand had felt in hers and how she had nearly led a boy to drown, and how hungry she is all the time now, and how restless. Almost.

Instead, she shakes her head and leans against the counter with Nixie, chewing as slowly as she's able to prolong their tentative intimacy and make this meal last.

12

Ceto sweeps into the bunker, her tail snapping along the floor. From the rim of the tube where they are gathered waiting, the sirens gaze up in welcome and shift to make room for her. But Ceto does not join them. Folding her tail beneath her, she pushes up onto one hip to preside over the sirens.

"One of your sisters has committed a violation of our trust," she says, as impassive as if she were ordering a shipment of fish.

Naia closes her eyes, preparing for her mother to expose her crimes and mete out the punishment she has been anticipating. Resentment eclipses the shame she knows she should feel. Her skin still tingles from the Pin Man's touch and her head is full of all the things she could have done—could still do—as Claire. Her mother has kept her from that life; cheated her of truly living. If Naia has betrayed Sirenland, her mother betrayed her first, and far worse.

Her aunts stare in silence at Ceto. She gives Nixie a chilling smile.

"Tell them what you have done," she orders.

Nixie shoots Naia a glare honed by fifteen years of resentment.

"You told her." Nixie's voice trembles with bewildered rage.

Naia blinks stupidly at her aunt. This is not about the boardwalk, then.

"I didn't say anything," Naia says. Nixie's eyes had cut to her across the bartender's cheek, demanding a pact of silence. "I promise I didn't!"

Ceto slaps her tail against the tiled floor. They fall silent.

"Nixie has used a man carnally in our theater."

The sirens stare at Nixie in incomprehension. She crosses her arms, her fingers digging into her elbows.

"I've done nothing worse than *she* has," Nixie spits at Naia. "Ask *her* where she goes at night, and who she fucks."

The accusation slams Naia, leaving her gasping, and she tries not to double over as her aunts turn their shocked faces to her.

"Naia?" Galene asks, concern flooding her eyes.

Naia shakes her head as Maris takes her hands, rubbing them as if to warm them.

"What's happened?" Maris asks gently. "Are you hurt?"

"Of course," Nixie sneers at them. "Poor Naia doesn't know any better. She's a victim of any man who looks at her, and I'm a slut who deserves what she gets. This is exactly why—"

"Enough." Ceto has no need to raise her voice. The word is like a whip. "Nixie will atone for her infidelity."

Nixie folds in on herself. Her eyes, deeply shadowed with purple paint, seem to sink in her pale face.

"It was a mistake," she whispers. "Please. I was upset."

She glances at Ceto with an accusatory look Naia can't interpret.

"And I was lonely. That girl's death made me so lonely I couldn't stand it."

Naia had never seen her aunt plead. It had never occurred to her that Nixie could be capable of vulnerability.

"We've all been lonely," Halia says gently.

"It's not the same." Nixie's eyes shimmer with tears. "You have Maris. Galene has Ceto, and Naia. You all have each another, but I—That girl died alone."

"We don't know she's dead." Halia takes her hand, smoothing her knotted fingers. "Let's not lose hope. And you must know we love you."

"You love each other more."

Halia turns her imploring gaze to Ceto.

"We all make mistakes," she says, trying and failing to meet Ceto's eyes. "I know I've done things I regret."

"Your past lives are irrelevant." Ceto is tranquil in her fury. "Nixie will leave us at once." She fixes her gaze on Naia in clear warning.

"What?" Halia whispers, as Galene says, "Oh, Ceto!" appealing to her for the first time. But Nixie's voice cuts through them in her anguish.

"Where would I go?" she beseeches her sisters, but they stare mutely back at her. She is shaking so hard her shell bracelets clack together. "Please—I'll do anything."

Although Naia had longed to be free of Sirenland for a night or two, to come and go as she pleased, she'd never imagined being banished from the only world she'd ever known. Who would she be without this place? Without her mother and aunts? As much as she wants to answer these questions for herself, she'd never considered leaving everyone and everything behind to do so. The idea of being cast out is petrifying. She clutches Maris's hands as if to tether herself.

"I've given you my life. I've helped make this place what it is," Nixie's voice turns shrill. "I've done everything you've asked of me and loved you like a mother. You won't so much as reprimand your daughter, but you'll cast me out?"

"You must reconsider," Galene appeals to Ceto as if in private.

"There is nothing I *must* do," Ceto says with an arch look at Galene. "But I will choose to be merciful. Nixie may have one chance to prove her loyalty: The mouth of the righteous is a well of life. If the sea wills for you to retain your sirenhood, she will guide you through the cliff and into the cove. Then, you may choose your path, whether it leads you away from us, or back to Sirenland."

"What kind of choice is that?" Galene demands. "That's a death sentence."

Ceto ignores her.

"Let this be a reminder to you all," she says. "There is no life beyond this one."

Nixie pulls her arms around herself as if gathering her sirenhood to her chest. She knows as well as Naia does that Ceto will not relent. Nixie lifts her chin with the insolence that made her a favorite with the Navy boys.

"I would expect no less from our mother," she says with false bravado. "And no worries—I'm a stronger swimmer than any of you."

As if daring those to be her last words, Nixie slips off the rim of the tube.

Banishment would be harrowing, but Naia cannot understand why Nixie would risk death rather than accept freedom, even if it meant leaving Sirenland behind for good. In a single night on the boardwalk she'd experienced more of the world than in her last fifteen years. How could choosing life be wrong? She dives after her aunts to escort Nixie into the tank. The curtains are shut.

The sirens cling to the rocks, their fins fluttering in the current that eddies out of the crack in the earth. The mouth of the sea tightens and disappears into darkness far below. As Nixie gulps from the hose snaking up from the oxygen tank, Ceto floats above them like an avenging angel.

She must love this place more than anything, if she's willing to destroy her family in service to it.

Naia takes Galene's hand as she had when she was a child.

Halia and Maris join them, forming a ring around the hole. Nixie plunges into the mouth of the sea with her arms outstretched, her tail thrashing against the current. As the tip of her fluke disappears into its depths, they bow their heads. Ceto leaves them to their vigil.

The sirens wait for as long as they have breath. When their need for air forces them to rise, they traverse Sirenland to the cove where the sea washes in and out of the fissure in the cliffside. Nixie does not come out.

13

Naia breathes in the brine-laced air at the clifftop. A line of patchy fir trees trembles in the wind. Hounded by chain restaurants, budget motels, and billboards for retirement communities, the road swerves around the cliff as if it can't get away fast enough. The parking lot across the road is full. Shingles are flaking off the roof of the clapboard building before her, and the mermaid sign that swings above the door is faded.

Naia's eyes are gummy from crying. Every time she turns her head, she expects to see Nixie and is struck anew by her death, unable to grasp the reality of this fresh horror. The moment Nixie disappeared into the black hole, time divided into Before and After, a clearly defined past and an uncertain future.

Far below, the sea lashes the walls of the cove and gulls toss themselves from the rocks. A foghorn sounds. Naia can still turn back. She can reclaim her worn-out role and be an obedient daughter, a blank-slate siren. But she would never learn the answer to the question the Pin Man posed to her; never figure out who she is and what she wants. Pushing forward may lead to her own banishment, even death, but turning back would mean a different kind of death.

Naia opens the door.

She is met by the scent of ruin, the breath of rotting ships exposed by the outgoing tide. She trails one hand against the damp wall of the staircase that descends into the cliff. At the bottom of the stairs, a curtain gives way to the bar. Its limestone walls weep with salt and the shag carpet stinks of mildew. A sour tang is baked into the air, mingling with a jumble of music and laughter. Above the tables an iron octopus hangs from a ceiling beam by one tentacle. Its seven other tentacles unfurl along the ceiling; their sucker bulbs emit the room's only light.

The cavernous room, draped in fishing nets, extends further back than Naia could see from the tank. Behind the bar, liquor bottles line a shelf along the observation window shrouded in heavy velvet curtains. A new bartender is mixing cocktails.

Naia shivers in the dank air and crosses her arms over her chest, concealing her peaked nipples. She understands so little about Sirenland; about her mother and how she had come to rule this place. The only story she knows is the one in which Ceto had entered the bar for the first and only time, in a borrowed dress. Had it looked anything like her own? The world slants a little. Naia reels past tables laden with plates of meat swimming in grease. She scans the guests, anticipating the Pin Man in every face, as if her will alone might summon him.

Her earlier encounters with him may have been colored by the thrill of transgression, but this is no longer about defiance; she *needs* to be Claire again, needs to make this sin against Sirenland worth the risk. It hadn't occurred to her that the Pin Man might break his word.

She sits at a small table squeezed between crowds of Navy boys where she'll be well hidden from her mother and aunts during the late-night show. The only other solitary figure in the bar is a man seated a few tables away. He stares at the curtain, gripping the sides of the table as if to tether it to the floor. His sharp face sags with extra flesh, and his neck slopes into his shoulders as if he were melting. He looks familiar, though Naia is certain she doesn't know him.

She folds her hands on the table and fixes her eyes on the curtain, ignoring the rowdiness at the neighboring tables. A crumpled napkin strikes her cheek and flutters into her lap. She flicks it away. Two of the Navy boys stand, cheered on by their friends, and Naia shrinks back in her seat, trying to make herself invisible.

One of the boys rests a palm on her table and leans in, searching out her gaze. She studies his bitten-down fingernails.

"What's a pretty thing like you doing in a place like this?" he asks, sliding his other arm around her shoulders, leaning in close enough for her to smell beer on his breath.

Naia meets his eyes, and he blinks back his insecurity. Is this the threat her mother and aunts had warned her about, this boy who can barely stand? Her mother would have torn him apart. *She* could tear him apart. She glares at the boy, conjuring the mysterious power that will grant her control over him. His eyes go fuzzy.

"There she is, destroyer of my heart," the Pin Man booms in his performer's voice, shoving through the boys toward Naia. The drinks he carries slosh down the glasses. She loses her hold on the boy as the Pin Man jostles him aside. In his black T-shirt and jeans and his assumed confidence, the Pin Man is conspicuous among the Navy boys. They toss a few halfhearted jibes at him and fade into the background.

Naia flushes with fury. How dare he assume she needed rescuing when she can save herself. As the Pin Man claims the seat beside Naia, his knee bumps hers under the table and he offers her his lopsided smile. She is annoyed by how quickly her anger turns to anticipation. He sets one of the glasses in front of her, and the candlelight plays across the pinpricks speckling his knuckles. Naia sips the drink to mask her interest in his hands. It burns on the way down. She can feel the heat from his skin through his jeans.

The Pin Man slides an olive from his toothpick with his teeth and chews, rolling the stick between his fingers, then pushes it into his cheek. He pulls it out again and runs it through the center of his chin.

"Am I supposed to ask how do you do that?" she asks.

He gives Naia his showman's wink and leans toward her as

if to whisper in her ear. Music grinds through the bar. He pulls away to watch the curtains rise and the Sirens' Theme begins.

We are not your average women
We're not yours to bed and keep
We want only to be swimmin'

A painted castle wavers in the background. Ceto descends from the conch shell, her hair unbound, her tail glittering with silver-tipped scales. Naia's aunts follow, their faces gleaming. They've adorned their temples and cheeks with Nixie's distinctive scales and divided her jewels among themselves. Their hair drips with paste diamonds. They clasp hands and sway before the window, mouthing the words.

We do not cook; we do not sweep
We are not your average women
We are sirens of the deep

Naia has never performed the late-night show and is surprised to find that rather than a story, it's an assortment of tricks designed to titillate: Halia peels and devours a banana, Maris downs a bottle of Coke in one luxurious gulp, Galene turns her back to the window and shimmies off her shells with a coy wink over her shoulder. Ceto dances with mysterious detachment, sensuous but self-contained. Without a plot, deprived of Nixie's flirtatious energy, the performance seems thin. The sirens gesture bigger and grin wider, trying to fill space.

Witnessing their sirenhood from this side of the tank, Naia is mesmerized. Their costumes smooth away the seam between skin and tail. The glass softens their features so they appear no older than Naia. They've disciplined themselves to withstand the cold and to maintain balletic control even when tugged this way and that by the current. Their bodies move with inhuman grace. These women are powerful. *She* is powerful.

For the first time, Naia sees what the audience sees, the magic she couldn't recognize while inside it. She'd thought the audience was enticed by the magic of their performance invoked by trickery: their tails, the props and backdrops, the jewels, the hidden air hoses. What makes the trickery believable is the kernel of truth at its core.

She scans the audience, eager to share her pleasure in the performance, but only the solitary man is watching. The Navy boys, and the occupants of the tables spanning all the way to the bar, are talking and laughing, drowning out the music, more interested in their food than the spectacle of real-live sirens. Not even the Pin Man is watching.

He's looking at Naia as the sirens undulate through the tank, pursing their lips and batting their lashes. For all their power, she is embarrassed for—embarrassed *of*—them, as they strive to seduce an indifferent room.

"What do you think?" she asks, challenging the Pin Man through Claire's eyes.

"They're beautiful," he says.

"You're not even looking."

"You're more beautiful," he says, his voice infused with stage bravado.

Every time she thinks she's gained the upper hand, he steals it out from under her. It's irritating—and exciting. She leans in to tell him what he can do with his compliments, but then, like a magic trick, he's holding her hand.

Unbidden, she recalls the man with his face pressed to the glass, slack-jawed in lust. Her palm sweats against the Pin Man's. She stares at her mother and aunts without seeing them, complicit in the audience's indifference.

• • •

Ceto saw Naia slip into the bar in a borrowed dress and leave with a man. Not even Nixie's death has curbed her daughter's defiance. She is failing Naia at every turn. Perhaps she would know how to be a good mother if she'd had a mother herself. But when she thinks "mother," all she can summon is the arctic cold—the same cold she felt when she'd realized Naia would never love her as much as she loved her daughter. It was an emptiness nothing could fill.

Her husband hadn't understood. When she'd tried to explain her grief, he'd just laughed and kissed her on the cheek and said, "She loves you—and I love you. I would be lost without you."

His version of love hadn't been what she'd expected, or wanted. It wasn't the thrilling, all-consuming love for which she'd cast off her tail. She'd thought it could be, at first, when he'd discovered her on the beach, tangled in the remnants of her tail. He'd wanted her with an urgency that had given her a sense of power. He'd done little things to show he cared. He knew she hated washing dishes and taking out the garbage, so he did those things. He brought her flowers on Valentine's Day and kissed her hello and goodbye. But the ease with which he professed his love made her doubt its integrity. Love couldn't be so easy. Her love for Naia was not easy. It was fraught and frightening, and far from calm.

She'd lain awake worrying and nursing Naia. She loved the heaviness in her breasts that eased as her daughter latched, and the swell of queasy devotion that released with the milk. It was a continued intimacy with her daughter long after Naia had left her body. But Naia began to need more, and nurse less. Her hunger was boundless. One night, Naia turned away from her breast, no longer dependent on her mother for sustenance. Her daughter didn't need her. Her husband didn't love her. If she was incapable of inspiring need, there must be something lacking in her. She'd come no closer to figuring out what would make her full.

When sirens grow restless, they follow the current to deeper waters. But this is where the current ended for Ceto. She was forgetting who she'd been before her body split apart to make way for Naia.

She lay beside her husband, her breasts and heart aching. She had to know if she could inspire love; if her husband needed her with the depth of emotion she longed to be needed with. Was it true he couldn't live without her? As he lay beside her she drew her fingernail just below his ear. She had never tasted him. She had not tasted anyone since she'd left the sea.

She touched her tongue to the blood that welled to the surface of his skin. As it slipped past her lips, she shuddered in response to a long-suppressed craving. His blood was so thick, richer than the wine she'd pretended was a satisfying substitute. Her desire roared back. She drank deep.

She tasted in his blood such sweet complexity: his boyhood in this house where he had grown up, his loyalty to this community, his deep belonging to this place. She tasted his pride and his gentleness and the steely confidence that had led him to take her because he wanted her, without questioning whether he deserved her.

She too had taken what she'd wanted when sirenhood had given her the right, but she had cast off that power with her tail. She'd quickly discovered that taking what she wanted didn't work for women. Motherhood, wifehood, was all giving. She missed taking.

She delved further, opening him deeper, seeking out his love for her. What rose up instead was his love for Naia, familiar in its immensity, but different than her own. He was free from the specter of loss that plagued her, the shadow-side of love. His love for Naia was simpler than hers.

Finally, she came to his love for her, lapping against the edges of everything else like a gentle wave. It was a calm, complacent love in which she saw herself reflected back to her as a calm, complacent woman. She had fit herself into his life and couldn't complain that she now held such a small place within it.

As she sucked at his inadequate blood, another taste rose to the surface. Something that filled her with such sharp longing that she pulled back, recognizing it for what it was when she met his eyes, wide with rich and delicious fear that overwhelmed all else. He was afraid of her.

His fear was stronger than his love for her or even Naia. Terror of death overrode all else. She held his eyes, savoring his horror because *she* had inspired it. She drank until it drained out of him, until Naia began to cry and brought her back to herself. She pulled away, sliding sticky across her husband's chest. His cold skin was now as white as the sheets on which they lay. His blank eyes pointed at the window.

She strapped her daughter to her chest and walked out to the cornfields. She walked until her bare feet were shredded as if by knives. She walked until she'd left her husband and the cornfields and the woman she'd been far behind. Her husband had called her "darling." Today, she took up her own name. She called herself Ceto.

14

Naia follows the Pin Man around the boardwalk gate where the sand gives way to a parking lot. It is nearly deserted now, and the pavement is cool beneath her bare feet. The Pin Man is silent, except for an occasional inhalation, as if he's trying to remember to breathe. She wants to take his arm as she had last night, but he walks ahead with his hands in the pockets of his jeans.

Beyond the parking lot, a narrow road bounded by tidy sidewalks curves along the ocean out of sight. A line of pastel hotels stand sentinel across the street. Their only windows face the ocean, as if their construction were left unfinished. Where the hotels end, motor inns and cottages crowd shoulder to shoulder.

Families pass Naia and the Pin Man with balloon swords and glow sticks. Just ahead, a man carries a little girl who rests her cheek on his shoulder and blinks back at Naia with heavy eyelids.

The Pin Man leads her through an alley between two cottages, crossing into an unruly landscape of vans and campers. Naia has the unsettling impression that the pastel road they had left behind was just a facade for this dingier world.

The Pin Man unlocks the door of a battered motorhome and ushers her up the steps. She tries not to betray her disappointment as she follows him inside, finding herself in a kitchenette with a two-burner stove and a mini fridge. Vinyl booths face each other across a laminate tabletop. Beyond the kitchenette, a narrow cot stands beside a half-open door through which she catches a glimpse of a toilet. The floor is sandy.

"I thought you'd live farther away," she says, standing in the middle of the room.

"Why?" the Pin Man asks, embarrassment softening his voice.

"Because you can." As the words leave her mouth, she suspects she's being rude. She pretends to be absorbed in her surroundings, hiding the flush she feels seeping up her cheeks.

The Pin Man's leather case rests on the table beside a photograph of a girl caught unaware, startled into a toothy smile. Naia picks up the photograph, studying the girl's baggy T-shirt, the protective lift of her shoulders, the bracelets stacked on one wrist.

"Who's this?" Naia asks.

The Pin Man folds his long frame into a booth.

"My wife," he says.

Naia sets the photograph down, trying not to jostle it, trying not to betray her confusing rush of jealousy and guilt and anger.

"You have a wife?" She sounds accusatory despite herself.

"Had," he says. "I had a house, too, and—" He sweeps his hand across his chest. "Button-up shirts."

He watches Naia, tugging at the nail in his ear. What had his wife thought of it? Had she grown tired of his attraction to pain and his resistance to straight answers? Naia has no frame of reference for this. She has never felt more like a little girl, never been more aware of her body: her arms dangling at her sides, her aroma of sweat and sea.

The Pin Man gazes up at her, as if waiting to be questioned, as if there's more she should want to know. When she doesn't speak, he fills the silence.

"We got married out of high school," he says, as if he'd been waiting to say these words. "She was pregnant."

Naia holds her breath, not daring to interrupt him. She slides into the booth across the table, wincing at the squeal of vinyl under her damp thighs.

"It was a hard pregnancy. I wanted her to take it easy, to stop working, but we needed the money. We didn't realize how sick she was." His voice tightens. He runs one thumb over his knuckles. His mouth twists, pulling at his cheeks.

"When she died, I didn't even lock the house," he says. "I took my uncle's RV and just started driving. I drove for months—until I found myself here."

He falls silent, staring down at his hands. Naia releases her breath as quietly as she can. She has never felt so helpless. His grief throbs between them, thick and impenetrable. She stares at the girl who had wrecked the Pin Man as thoroughly as a storm at sea.

"I'm sorry," she says. It's the only thing she can think to say. He shrugs, donning his performer's bravado again.

"Don't be. I've got a promising career and pretty young fans." He waggles an eyebrow at her. "And with all the pain I've been through, my skin's tougher than leather."

He'd gone deep for a moment, but had already pulled back, denying her his depths. She's tired of people withholding from her, treating her like a child who can't handle their truths. Her aunts' half-shared lives, her mother's existence before Sirenland, Naia's own father. She traces the locks of the leather case, luring the Pin Man's eyes to her roving fingers. When he doesn't stop her, she flips the lid, exposing the red satin studded with pins.

"Show me," she says, holding out a pin.

He accepts it, careful not to touch her fingers, and presses his hand palm-down on the table. The bell trills as he slides the pin between his first two knuckles.

Naia plucks another pin from the cushion and, when he nods, nudges it between his second two knuckles. The skin gives way like sand. She tries a third pin against her pinky. When the steel holds firm, she pushes harder until it punctures her skin. Blood wells at her fingertip. The Pin Man places his hand over hers.

"They're real," she says.

The Pin Man gives her a half-smile that doesn't reach his eyes. He never fully smiles. He never flinches.

"What did you expect?" he asks, lifting one shoulder in a shrug.

She'd expected trickery, a fantasy woven around a kernel of reality. She hadn't imagined that he would use performing to hide from his true self, as Ceto and her aunts do—as she does. Until now, Naia hadn't thought of sirenhood as a front for her true self, if there even is anyone else beneath the role she was born to play. She'd expected him to be different, for showmanship to be one of many adventures, along with wrestling alligators and sleeping under the stars, a stop along the road of his rich, intrepid life before he moved on to someplace more interesting. This couldn't just be where he ended up.

Naia catches his gaze until the fuzzy look comes into his eyes. She leans into him, breathing in his astringent scent. She wants to know who he is—who he really is—and since he won't show her, she'll find out herself.

With unsteady fingers, she presses the pin to the flesh below his ear and draws a line of blood to the surface of his skin. He makes a sound, as if starting to speak, but she glances up at him again, catching his eyes, lulling him back into submission.

Naia slides her lips against his neck, where his skin is warm and salty. His pulse jumps against her mouth. His blood soaks between her lips and she gags on the rusty bite of it. A hint of richness emerges beyond her grasp, like from the fog-cloaked sea. She reaches toward it, yearning to understand.

In the fog she sees, or tastes, or *feels* something tight and pulsing. She pushes deeper, deeper still, until she touches a knot of self-loathing veined with despair. She strains toward it, tearing into it to find coiling there a torment she'd never known the human body could withstand. His shame and grief seeps toward her, oozes around her seeking a way in. Naia breaks away with a gasp.

The Pin Man slumps back on the bench. His eyes are closed. His skin is white. Naia presses her knuckles against her mouth, grinding the taste of him from her lips. Blood smears down his neck and trickles into the collar of his shirt. She reaches out to him and at the sight of her own blood-tipped fingers pulls away, afraid his skin will be as cold as it looks. Through her panic, she becomes conscious of a slight movement: his chest rising and falling. She hears herself make a sound caught between a sob and a laugh.

Naia wipes the pin clean, its bell plinking with the shaking of her hands, and slides it back into its place in the cushion. The Pin Man's blood lingers on her tongue. He can keep his pain.

15

Naia strips off her dress, damp with the Pin Man's blood, and stuffs it into the bag. Her stomach groans, unsatisfied. She has come no closer to understanding power. Her dominance over the Pin Man had been nauseating rather than empowering, and had taught her nothing about herself.

She does not know what is hidden in her own secret depths, although worse than punishment, worse than being confined to Sirenland forever, worse than submitting to her mother's rule for the rest of her life, would be to discover there's nothing there at all. Just an empty space, a gnawing hunger she can never satisfy. Naia plunges into the surf, willing the sea to wash away her restlessness along with the Pin Man's blood.

She stows her bag and flows into the tunnel. Instead of returning to the room she shares with her mother, she branches off, following the passage she knows leads to Ceto's throne room. She emerges into the room, empty but for Ceto's throne and her spare tail hanging from a hook.

Like Ceto's tail and shells and crown, her throne is unadorned, built to serve a function. Naia runs her fingers along the lacerations in its arms. She'd watched her mother gouge her fingernails through the wood while smiling at guests in the photo line.

What's one more transgression? Naia climbs onto the seat. Its edge presses into the backs of her bare knees. There is no padding, like on her own throne, and those of her aunts, but the wood is cool against her hot skin. She tips her head back against the throne and waits, hoping for some kind of transformation, *a sea-change into something rich and strange.* As if by taking her mother's place she might absorb something of her boldness to face the confrontation she knows is coming. She ignored Ceto's final warning; her mother will punish her this time, and it will be severe. Naia can't begin to imagine how to prepare herself. She cannot fathom leaving Sirenland for good.

Shivering with apprehension and unmet hunger, Naia slips into the hallway and holds her breath as she passes her bedroom and her aunts' room, on to the kitchen. The click of the door echoes in the tunnel. She pulls it shut behind her and only then releases her breath. The steel appliances gleam in the moonlight. The lingering scent of grease clogs the air. She tugs open the refrigerator and breathes in the blast of cold that shocks her heated flesh.

Her stomach groaning with need, Naia swipes the foil from plates and yanks the lids from plastic containers. She dips her fingers into them, scooping their contents into her mouth. Salty and sweet and sour mingle on her tongue, slide down her throat. She eats until her jaw aches, but hunger still yawns inside her.

Naia leans back against the refrigerator, prickling her bare skin. Her body betrays her, unable to satisfy itself. She is still empty. The sun is rising and her mother will soon be awake. Naia will not wait to be summoned. She has learned that much about power.

Ceto is seated on the edge of the oyster shell in a robe that stops short of her knees. Her slim legs emerge from the hem and taper to delicate ankles. Her feet skim the seawater rippling around the bed. She holds her tail across her lap, its razor black scales glittering. Naia's tail is not on the hook where she'd left it.

Naia steels herself for her mother's rage. She suppresses the impulse to cover her nakedness with her hands and lifts her chin in defiance she had learned from Nixie. If she must leave, she will do so with dignity. Even still, tears gather in her eyes and she locks her knees to stop their shivering.

"I'd like to say goodbye to my aunts," she says, her voice quavering despite herself.

Ceto rises before her, and Naia is surprised by how small her mother is. She'd always had the impression that she towers over all others, but Naia is taller than her mother, she realizes with a sense of vertigo. Ceto wades through the waves that glow like fire from the sun rising beyond the window. She comes to a stop before Naia, so close her skin heats the sliver of air between them, and whispers, "I smell blood on you."

Naia's breath catches. Her mother regards her not with the anger she'd anticipated, but with an unfamiliar expression that creases her forehead and casts fine wrinkles in the corners of her eyes. Naia had been braced for battle, but her mother's serenity leaves her reeling. She sinks to the edge of the shell. Her mother kneels at her feet. The folds of her robe part, and Naia looks away from her animal center as Ceto takes her hands, engulfing them in her palms.

"You are hungry," her mother says gently.

Naia nods, and her tears spill over. How she has longed to be understood by someone—but to be understood by her mother is terrifying. Still, she leans into her mother's touch, seeking warmth and reassurance, even as she knows Ceto is incapable of offering such comfort.

"The hunger will grow stronger," Ceto says. "You will hurt people, and they will fear you. This is a dangerous world for frightening women."

"Why must I be frightening?" Naia asks, clutching her mother's hands.

"Because the alternative is to be frightened. You and I—we fear neither men nor monsters. *We* are the monsters."

What Naia had felt with that boy, with the Pin Man, snaps into place. There is something wrong with her. Something that renders her unfit for the world beyond Sirenland. She finally understands that Sirenland isn't here to protect her, it's here to protect the world *from* her.

"The savagery that makes us feared beyond these cliffs makes us desired within them," Ceto says. "We harness our power through performance."

Naia's mother holds her own tail open. Naia stares down into the fabric pooling between them, glittering in the sunlight that streams through the window.

"I built Sirenland for you," Ceto says. "It is time you claim it."

Naia closes her eyes, casting deep inside herself. She expects to find relief; she has evaded punishment, and need no longer steel herself for the unimaginable. But she isn't relieved. She is disappointed. She had wanted something to happen; maybe she wanted to be forced out of Sirenland because she doesn't have the courage to leave on her own.

Shaking, Naia slides her legs into her mother's tail.

• • •

Naia waits alone at the rim of the tube. Her mother's black tail disappears into the black water and she flips her fluke to reassure herself that it's still there. The sheath hugs her flesh in some places and sags in others where it had molded to Ceto's body. The seam between her stomach and tail is expertly designed to fade from skin to scales, erasing the evidence of her humanity.

Naia gathers her breath and slips into the tube, welcoming the cold surging up her spine. Hand over hand, she pulls herself down into the tank and takes her mother's place as the final siren to greet the sea.

Power flows through her, from beyond her fingertips through her arms and torso and the tail that is part of her in a way her old tail had never been, lengthening her so she becomes a wave within the waves.

Performing has always been second nature to Naia, as natural to her as breathing. She had never thought of it as having a function. She focuses inward, seeking out the hunger. It's there, simmering just beneath the surface. She recoils from its intensity, pushing her body into an arabesque that feels forced and stiff. The hunger licks at her ribs, insistent.

She gives into it, just a little, allowing it to gather and spread. She closes her eyes, sending her focus deep down into it, and slowly begins to direct it. The ache flows through her, into her muscles, her ribs, building and building until with a single thrash of her tail she propels halfway across the tank to her waiting aunts, accompanied by a blaze of elation.

Naia comes up short before an unfamiliar stage set: a palace interior constructed of crystal and coral. Clamshell windows open with a fizz of bubbles. A ceiling of anemones billows in the current; from it hangs a pearl chandelier.

In a castle fine as glass, three sirens rule the sea. The eldest sisters are content with their kingdom, but the youngest yearns for more. Her days are dark with silt, and unchanging. Her hunger is boundless. She longs for her every cell to be suffused with lust and love. She wants to be full.

A shadow passes over the palace, and as the youngest siren, Naia looks up, pantomiming wonder as the surface explodes into shattering colors, a celebration the likes of which she has never seen.

Her sisters tell her that no good can come of longing, but she pays them no heed. As she ventures toward the surface, the waves try to face her down. She pushes on.

Lightning splits the sea and Halia, in the prince's leggings and billowing white shirt, crashes through the surface and plummets toward the black hole, trailing a ribbon of blood.

The siren cannot bear to watch the prince drown. Ignoring her sisters, whose warnings are whipped away by the waves, she wraps her arms around the prince's waist and bears him to her palace, where she lays him down in her garden of seagrass and strokes his pale cheeks.

With a crack of thunder that chatters the chandelier, Ceto the sea witch comes to her, offering magic for a price—but the siren can invoke her own magic now. Her sisters despair as she slices her palm with her teeth and lifts the prince's face to the gauze of her blood. Trembling, he opens his eyes to Ceto's daughter.

The siren grants the prince his life and fulfills his every wish; all that she asks in return is that he never return to the surface. They reign together in the sea, where a century passes in a single day.

The prince is content—until one fateful evening, when a shadow drifts over the palace. He looks up, remembering the storm that had brought him to this world. He is overcome with desire to see his kingdom just once more.

Compelled by a yearning for home more powerful than the fealty he has sworn to the siren, he rises through the sea and breaks the surface. There, he sees a ship the likes of which he has never seen, and the landscape so changed he cannot be certain it is the one he left. This is no longer his world.

The prince dives back into the waves but finds that he cannot breathe below the surface. The siren rails against him for his betrayal, but she cannot let him go. She draws the prince back down to their palace, thwarting his desperate struggle. He loses his fight for breath before they reach the coral gates.

The siren binds him to the garden floor with a rope of bull kelp and holds vigil as the days pass in unceasing twilight. She loves him long after the flesh has fallen from his bones.

When the curtain shuts, Naia slices through Halia's bindings, releasing her to the waves. They join the others at the mouth of the spring and bow their heads.

Naia closes her eyes in prayer, finally understanding why her mother insists on this ritual—finally understanding the intensity and severity of Ceto's sirenhood. Her mother created this kingdom to curb their terrible need and laws to ensure they do no harm. She thanks the sea for offering her a way to tame her hunger. It's still there, gnawing at her insides, but it's calmer now, its fury expended in the best performance of her life.

16

Naia flows up the tube after her aunts and emerges into the bunker, struck by a sudden silence. The only sound is the water dripping from the sirens' hair onto the tiled floor. Around the rim of the tube, her aunts wear mirror images of shock. Even Ceto's ruthless face is drained of color.

A man stands before them. His boots have tracked muddy prints across the floor. Although he towers above the sirens, he looks as though his body had once taken up more space and has since shrunk down to the bone. He carries himself like a more imposing man and seems to fill the room with his uneasy intensity.

Naia has seen him before. At the bar last night—and before that, being led away by the bartender. He had pounded on the glass.

Her breath catches with sudden awareness of their vulnerability. Their legs are bound; it would be easy for this man to do anything he wanted to them.

The sirens stare up at him, shifting closer together. His face reddens, his lips twist.

"What—" Ceto begins, and even she startles when the man falls to his knees.

He buries his face in Galene's lap with a hoarse cry. Pressing his lips to her palms, he clutches her fingers until they're white. She turns her face away, squeezing her eyes shut.

"Dolly! I thought you were dead. I'd given up—but then you were right there, on the news."

The reporters. The cameras. Death had brought this man to Sirenland; *Claire* had brought him here.

"What happened to you?" He takes Galene's face between his hands, engulfing her cheeks in his broad palms. "What happened to—" He rakes his eyes over the sirens, as if searching for something, and his gaze catches on Naia.

"Is this her?" he asks, his voice thick with emotion Naia can't place. He reaches for her, and when she shifts away, he falls back heavily. His eyes glitter with tears.

"She's beautiful," he says. "God, Dolly, she's so beautiful."

"She's not yours," Galene whispers.

He flinches as if struck. A spark of anger ignites behind his eyes.

"Whose?"

"She's not mine, not ours. We don't have a child."

"I don't understand. I don't—you were pregnant. When you disappeared, you were—"

"I told you," Galene says. The words catch in her throat, but she forces them out. "I *told* you it wasn't what I wanted. I told you I didn't want a child. I couldn't sleep, couldn't *breathe*. I felt like I was dying."

His knees slip on the wet tiles and he catches himself with his hands, crouching before her.

"What did you do?" His voice is a rasp of pain.

Galene shakes her head, her lips tight and trembling. His hands clench into fists.

"What did you *do*?" He pounds one thigh with a heavy fist and Galene flinches, as if out of habit.

The sirens pull closer together, pinning Galene between them, shielding her from the force of his mounting fury. Her shoulders curve to protect her chest, and Naia pushes her fingers through her aunt's. Galene's hands are cold. Ceto's eyes have not left her face.

"Would it have been so awful to bear our child?" He chokes on the words.

"Yes." Her voice is small but firm.

His mouth slackens in dumb hatred.

"All that time, I was looking for you and you were just . . . here? With these—*women*," he says, sneering at Maris.

Ceto tears her eyes form Galene and her spine snaps straight as if she could rise above this man made feral by grief.

"You will go now," she commands him.

He rounds on her with a look that had likely cowed many others, but Ceto holds him until a dazed look comes into his eyes.

"Stop," Galene says, acknowledging for the first time Ceto's unspoken power. She shakes her head, the slightest gesture. "It's not your place."

Ceto's lips peel back over her teeth. As Naia now knows, there is nothing as insulting as being made vulnerable. Still, her mother releases the man from her thrall. He staggers back.

"What was that?" he asks, alarm heightening his voice.

"I'm sorry." Galene releases Naia's hand and takes his with obvious reluctance. "I'm sorry, but it was a long time ago. Please, just go."

"What's going on here?" He glares at Ceto. "What have you done to my wife?"

Ceto struggles to maintain her serene expression as Galene tugs at his hand, tearing his attention back to her.

"You didn't even know how to swim," he says with a harsh laugh. "You're too scared—of everything. You wouldn't even fuck with the lights on. Do you really think men want to watch you, half-naked, pretending to be a *mermaid*?" he spits as if it's a curse. "You're making idiots of yourselves, all of you."

Galene shrinks away from him. Struck by the ugliness of his words, Naia recognizes her breathless horror reflected on her aunts' faces, on her mother's face, as if for the first time, her mask has slipped. The woman beneath it is tired and scared, held together by sheer will and the conviction that she is something more than herself. Humiliation—for all of them—brings the taste of blood to the back of Naia's throat.

"Get up," he orders Galene.

Her eyes cast down, fixed on her tail, she says, "No."

He digs his fingers into her arm. She tries to jerk away, but he twists her arm behind her, and she gasps in pain as he wrenches her to her knees.

Naia acts without thought, driven by instinct. She slams her tail into his ankles, and he drops, scrambling for purchase on the tiles. Before he can catch his breath, she grasps his thick arm with both hands and yanks him into the tube. Water closes over Naia's head, cutting off Galene's cry.

Although she has the benefit of surprise, the man is heavy. He pummels blindly at her, and a sudden jerk brings them up short as he clutches a handhold, staying them against the current. Ropes of muscle strain along his arms.

Naia sinks her teeth into his hand and he releases the bar. She yanks him through the tube, trailing blood behind them. As they emerge into the tank, the man's boot connects with Naia's temple, blinding her with pain. Galene flows into the space between them, shielding Naia from his desperate rage.

He clamps one arm around Galene's neck in an alligator grip, towing her down with him as Naia claws at his face, shredding his cheeks. He drives a fist at Naia, pushing through the sea's resistance, and as it grazes her chin she feels their eyes lock. His arms fall, pinned at his sides. Maris and Halia swoop past them to gather Galene and rush her back to the surface.

Her mother's blood boiling through her, Naia tests her connection to the man now gaping at the end of her line. It holds firm, and she hauls him toward the black hole as hunger twists in her gut, in her head, suffuses her with need. Blind with hunger, she sinks her teeth into the meat between his shoulder and neck and bears down until her teeth scrape bone.

She clings to him, drunk on the pungent fury of his blood. Within it is a strain of something familiar: a sour and desperate resentment mingled with metallic love, the rotting sweetness of loss.

Ceto pulls up behind him, her eyes blazing at Naia over his head. Their eyes hold, meeting hunger with hunger, and a current of understanding flows between them. She recognizes in her mother's eyes a challenge, a desire for Naia to succumb to her ravenousness; to do in Sirenland what is forbidden beyond it. *Go on*, her mother wills her as loudly as if she'd screamed it. *Give in. Take what you want. This man is of no consequence.*

Shock stalls Naia's pounding hunger and her mind clears as if released from a spell. Ceto watches her eagerly, her eyes glittering with anticipation. Naia's last illusions fall away and she sees the truth of this place. Ceto didn't make Sirenland for her daughter. She created this world for herself, where she can wield absolute power. She's come to think she can manipulate everyone around her, even control life and death without consequence. In this moment, Naia sees her mother more clearly than ever before, and her self-delusion is terrifying.

The man is heavy in Naia's arms, entirely at her mercy. His life hangs on whether she embraces or denies her mother's legacy. The man opens his eyes to her. She knows what he sees. Naia is beautiful. She is so fair her veins run beneath her skin like water under ice. Her blue-black hair is thick as rope, her eyes gray as the stormy sea. He could lose himself in them.

But she will not be responsible for this man's death. She pushes him at Ceto and swims for the tube without looking back.

Ceto coils around the man's waist, constricting her scales until his face bulges. His bruised gut swells below her muscled tail. She fits against him, sliding along his belly, and presses her barnacled breasts against his chest. His flesh tears beneath her fingernails. She drives her mouth into his, reveling in his complex taste.

The bloodlust of her birthright returns to her. His chest caves under hers as the final gasp of breath leaves his body. She sinks her teeth deeper, until she tastes blood, and rips off his bottom lip.

Some drowning, still-sane part of her sends up a warning, but she is tired of holding back. She is ravenous, and Naia has abandoned her. She no longer has reason to hold back. Ceto rolls the man down through a red fog and into the hole where she devours him, choking down every last bit of his humanity.

17

Naia opens the door to the motorhome without knocking. The interior is dark except for a light above the table where the Pin Man sits reading.

"Hey!" His eyebrows lift and he sets his book on the table.

The violence of the man's fingers twisting in her hair has broken something open in her, unleashing an unanchored anguish. She'd turned away from the man in the tank. She will not become a monster. She will not just take what she wants just because she can. She doesn't know what she wants or who she wants to be—she just knows she doesn't want to be like Ceto, and that means she must leave Sirenland.

She stands before the Pin Man with the taste of another man's blood on her lips.

"Do you like me?" she demands.

The Pin Man's eyes flicker over her face.

"Of course I like you," he says, chafing his fingers across his knuckles.

"But not because I want you to, right? You like me because . . . because I'm likable?" She flushes at her brazenness, but presses on.

The Pin Man is the one person who knows her as someone other than the role her mother forced her on her, the one person who sees her as a normal girl. Leaving Sirenland wouldn't be so scary if they escape together. She could start a new life with him, as Claire.

Naia gathers a breath.

"And if you were to kiss me, it would be because you *want* to kiss me, and not because I want you to?"

He looks up at her, confusion tugging at his lips.

"*Do* you want me to?" he asks.

She growls in frustration, balling her fists as if to pummel him.

"Okay, okay!" he says with a showman's laugh. "Of course I want to kiss you."

"Then do it," she says.

The Pin Man slides out from behind the table to stand before her. He leans in, and she closes her eyes. She feels his lips brush her forehead, gentle, quivering with control.

She is tired of his control—and her own. She reaches down between them, finding the hilt of his dagger, and tugs it free from its sheath. It has no folds, no secret compartments. It's solid and sharp, deadly in its ordinariness. She presses its point beneath his chin. But he just stands there, staring dumbly at her.

"Kiss me like you're drowning. Kiss me until you taste blood," she demands.

He drops his hands from her shoulders and takes a step back.

The rejection leaves her breathless, her eyes burning. She could make him want her. She could make him kiss her like he meant it—but she would know the difference. She can't arouse passion without force; she can only bend others to her will and make them mute before her, like fish gaping at a hook. Her lungs tighten as they never have beneath the waves. She wonders if it's possible to drown on land.

She doesn't want to be like her mother who forces people to do what she wants. She will not give into her monstrousness by creating a small world for it to exist within.

The Pin Man reaches for her hand and meets her eyes with a level gaze, as if willing her to read his mind.

"I do want you, Naia."

His words shoot a bolt of queasy relief through her stomach. And then their meaning sinks in.

"You knew?" To her mortification, her eyes fill with tears. "You knew who I was this whole time and you let me pretend to be someone else?"

She's been made ridiculous, having paraded herself as Claire before an audience who was in on the joke. She had never held his attention with her simple human self.

"I understand wanting to become someone else," he says. "But I need you to know that I like *you*, Naia, for who you are, not who you pretend to be."

"How can you say that? You don't even know me."

He takes her hand tentatively, as if expecting her to strike him.

"You're the reason I came to Sirenland—to see the Aquatic Infant everyone was talking about. I just stopped in for a drink, but as I watched you, I felt hopeful for the first time in months. I came to the show again and again and stayed, for you. It was enough just to see you. I never expected to meet you, or to . . . to like you as much as I do."

His words crash around her without meaning. He's ripped Claire down the middle, killed her again. Poor Claire, she grieves as she tears away from that scowling girl with her hands thrust in the pockets of her dress, her damp collarbones, her ponytail coming loose from its rubber band, crackling in the heat, her nails painted like a rainbow, her scent of bug spray and her dirty toes, a preening seagull before an indifferent audience. He had never liked her; only ever Naia, and even then, just the postcard version. Like everyone else, he'd been enchanted by the role she'd been born into, without agency, the trickery woven around the sad truth that there is no other self at the heart of her performance. Not yet.

"But . . . if you liked me before you even met me, then you don't like me for myself. You like me for who you thought I was and who you wanted me to be, who my mother made me into—and who *I* wanted you to think I was."

He grasps her shoulders, shaking his head in confusion, but she persists.

"You liked the version of me I manipulated you into wanting by performing what I thought you'd want."

"That makes no sense," he says. "I do know you!"

"The person you think you know is just another performance." She glares into his eyes, hating him for his false love and for stripping Claire from her, and because she will always be empty whether she stays in Sirenland or goes with him—and so she must go alone and that is terrifying. She hates the part of herself that had welcomed the bondage of her tail. And she is hungry; so furiously hungry. She doesn't need this damaged man, full of holes, to help her understand herself.

"Thanks for the knife," she says, and shuts his door behind her.

• • •

Ceto waits for the change to come, welcoming the pain. Her hunger had not been spent in the man's sacrifice; it pushes out against her uncomfortably swollen stomach. Her legs are slick inside her second-best tail. She waits for the ache to bloom inside her, for the pressure to grind into her center. She wonders if it will hurt more than when she had split her tail into legs, more than when Naia had rent her apart in birth. She will hurt this final time, and then she will never hurt again.

She'd made that promise before.

The night she left her husband cold in their bed, Ceto hadn't even stopped to change her blood-streaked nightgown, or pack a bag. All she had was Naia.

She'd carried her sleeping daughter to the road and waited for the first bus that pulled up. She didn't care where it was going. Her knowledge of the world was limited to this one dusty town where the gas station also served as the grocery store and post office. Anywhere would be better than here.

As Ceto folded into a seat at the back of the bus, the sun was just beginning to rise, peering up over the horizon edge of highway. Naia whimpered, and Ceto tugged down the neck of her dress, girding herself for the rush of nausea that accompanied the release of milk. She rested her forehead against the window, staring out at the flat earth as Naia suckled back to sleep. If they kept moving, Ceto figured they'd reach the sea eventually. She didn't know what they would do when they got there.

As they traded one bus for the next, the land shifted from coarse brown to green made vibrant by the relentless sun. Time smeared by, and Ceto moved in and out of sleep. She was back in her husband's bed, made hot by his desire. Back further still, tangled in her dreams like the fishing net that had once hauled her thrashing from the sea, trapped among a writhing mass of fish, to be dumped on a ship's deck. She'd slain the fishermen before they'd recovered from their shock and slid through their hot blood to freedom. As she'd returned to the sameness of the sea, she'd wondered for the space of a single breath what it would have been like to succumb to capture.

Ceto awoke surrounded by strangers. She drifted back to sleep and when she woke again, they were gone, replaced by other strangers. She became familiar with diners, where she only ever ordered a plain waffle and green tea that reminded her of the ocean. Everything else made her stomach roil. She collected travel brochures from the racks at the diners and bus stops, and pored over them in the halo of the bus's overhead light. Even the smallest towns—the ones they passed through on the way to real destinations—had their attractions: a state fair that boasted the world's largest butter sculpture, a hair museum, a sinkhole, a reenacted colonial village, a UFO campground. When the brochures began to promote surfing and water parks, Ceto knew they must be close.

She refolded the brochure for Sirenland, kingdom of "Live Mermaids!," which she'd studied until the creases frayed and the pages began to separate. Beyond the photos of performers grinning in whimsical tails, Ceto perceived a world of women, powerful athletes thriving in sisterhood. She tucked the brochure into her pocket for safe keeping.

Naia stirred and Ceto rested a palm on her daughter's warm back, pressed her lips to the top of her head, where the hair swept into a double cowlick like her father's. Ceto would never speak his name again. She wouldn't even think of him, except to put more, ever more distance between them; between herself and the woman she used to be. She would be enough for Naia.

Ceto awoke to something sliding up her bare thigh. The man

beside her had a round, pink face at odds with his crisp Navy uniform. His hand stalled against her skin. They both looked down at it, as if surprised. Naia stirred against her breast.

"It's okay," he murmured, resettled his hand and petting her thigh as if calming a cornered animal. "You look like you could use some company." He slid her dress higher, scraping his finger along the edge of her underwear.

The force of her revulsion struck her like a kick in the gut. How dare this man think he can take what he wants, and that she'd freely give it to him. She caught his eyes, which were small and too close together, and gave him the board-buckling glare that had felled a thousand ships.

"Remove your hand," she commanded him.

As he jerked his hand away, alarm leapt in his eyes. She could smell it on him, heady and rich. She leaned closer, breathing it in. Her hunger flared. The waffle she'd choked down hours before hadn't been satisfying, even then, and this man's blood, suffused with fear and gluttonous lust, was a temptation she couldn't fight. Nor should she have to—he was a bad man who didn't deserve exoneration. Her husband hadn't been a bad man, but she pushed that thought aside.

Ceto skimmed her fingernail down the side of his neck. His blood welled at the skin and slipped down into his uniform collar. She sucked the fear from her fingertip.

"What's going on?" a voice behind them asked. Another man

in a Navy uniform leaned over the seat, interrupting their locked gaze.

The man beside Ceto lurched away from her, clutching his hand to his neck.

"She did something to me." His panicked squeak was so satisfying that she laughed in his face.

"What?" his friend asked, leaning closer.

"I dunno—" He stared at his hand as if mesmerized by the sight of his own blood.

"This bitch thinks she's tough," the man behind her growled, though she detected a waft of fear in his breath.

"You have no idea," Ceto said, but before she could pin him with her gaze, something sharp bit into her side of her neck. She pressed her hand against Naia, sleeping still against her chest.

"Apologize to my friend," said the man with the knife.

She was a siren, a queen, a killer. She did not apologize. She was not sorry. She tried to shake her head but the steel bit into her skin, then slid down her neck to Naia's cheek.

Her gaze flittered around the bus like a trapped bird. The handful of scattered passengers wore Navy uniforms. She caught one man's eye across the aisle, and he gave her a shit-eating grin and deliberately turned his head to the window.

Beside her, the man's fingers stuttered up her thigh again, and squeezed until she bit her lip to keep from crying out.

"Apologize," he said.

The knife glinted against her sleeping daughter's cheek.

"I am sorry," she said through clenched teeth.

"You can do better." He unzipped his trousers with jittering fingers, avoiding her eyes.

The knife pressed against the back of her neck, guiding her down. Bile rose in her throat as she slid to her knees on the gritty floor. Her shoulders wedged against the back of the next seat. In this moment, she vowed that if she left this bus alive, she would never be used by men again. She would humble them instead, every chance she got.

"Next, you'll apologize to my friend for making him threaten you," he said, his voice quavering as he shifted to release himself from the stiff fabric of his trousers.

His friend tapped his knife on the seatback as he groaned into her unwashed hair.

Ceto willed Naia not to wake. She fixed her eyes on one of the gold buttons of his jacket, holding her breath against the ripe stink of him, and lifted her chin. As he forced himself down her throat, she longed to bite through layers of tissue and nerve, to hear him scream as she devoured the inconsequential part of this man that made him believe he had power over her.

Dirt ground into her kneecaps but she was caught tight between the seats and the man's fingers flexed in her hair. She was nothing more to him than a mouth. While he grunted and thrust his hips, driving himself deeper into her, she pretended she *was* just a mouth, just a hole, empty and incapable of pain or humiliation. A caught hair twisted against the roof of her mouth. When he came with a nauseating shudder, she spat his semen between his feet where it turned gray with dirt.

She closed her eyes, gathering herself for whatever came next—but the bus groaned to a stop, and to her relief, the man zipped his trousers. Without a word, he lifted his leg over her and stepped into the aisle. His friend fell in line with the rest of the men as they strode off the bus.

Ceto waited between the seats, holding her breath until the bus released a gasp of exhaust and began to move again. Her tongue felt thick. She wondered if she would feel better if she cried. She rested her cheek on the worn vinyl and looked down at her daughter. Naia's eyes were open.

Ceto wraps her arms around her stomach. The tank light pools around her, shifts over her, strokes her where she lies on the spring floor listening to her heartbeat, until she can no longer bear to be contained.

She makes her way through Sirenland and into the cove, craving the open sea. She invites the current to carry her where it wills, welcoming the thrashing of the waves. Rendered to base animal instinct, Ceto gives in to her body, waiting to be cleaved from the inside, for her legs to seal.

When her lungs are tight to burning, she rises to the surface, gasping and cursing herself for her dependence on air.

"Sisters!" she screams, clawing at the net. "Sisters!"

They come quickly, as though they'd been waiting.

"You lied to me." Ceto bites back a sob of humiliation.

"You know we do not lie." Their black eyes absorb the darkness and reflect nothing back.

"Then why have I not transformed?" she demands. "I have made a sacrifice, and yet I remain human."

They look at each other, feigning incredulousness.

"Now she wants what we have offered." They laugh with the sound of bones snapping. "As if she had not shunned us, twice."

Need ravages Ceto from the inside with the redoubled force of an addiction revived. Naia rejected her love and the life Ceto had created for her. Galene lied to her. Nixie is gone, and Sirenland is imploding around her. She'd lost control somehow. There is nothing left for her but to return to the sea, to absolute power and oblivion, to be ruled by simple hunger.

"Tell me." Her gut twists, and she loses herself in the fathomless dark of their eyes. "Please."

"We said a *sacrifice*, not a self-serving murder." Her sisters' voices drip with scorn. "A kill is not a sacrifice if it means nothing to you."

They lean close to Ceto across the net.

"A true sacrifice breaks your heart."

18

Ceto finds Galene waiting in her throne room, dressed in the starched uniform she had arrived in so long ago. The fabric hangs on her now. She bows her head before Ceto, her eyes downcast at her orthopedic shoes.

"I'm leaving," she says.

Ceto slides into her throne, tracing her sharp fingernails along the grooves she's carved into the arms.

"Bathe me first," she commands.

Galene kneels before her, deftly finding her seam with shaking fingers. Her hair is piled on her head in a messy knot, revealing the nape of her neck where fine gray hairs stick to her skin.

Galene shudders as Ceto traces her thumbs up the ridge of her spine. It would be easy to dig her nails into the soft base of her skull and hold Galene's face in her lap until her breath stops.

She allows Galene to tug her tail down her thighs, revealing welts where the fabric has depressed her flesh, tattooing the imprint of scales across her skin. Her legs ache when freed, but she barely registers the pain.

While Galene retrieves the bucket and sponge from the water closet, Ceto stands and dons her robe. Uncertain, Galene waits before her.

"Sit, please." Ceto gestures to her throne. It is not an invitation.

Galene lowers herself to the seat, and allows Ceto to strip her shirt over her head and her saggy skirt from her waist until she is naked on the throne. Ceto appraises her body. It had long ago lost its roundness and uncertainty, but Dolores is still there in her eyes.

Ceto draws the sponge from the bucket and applies it to Galene's temples and her careworn curves, cleansing her for sacrifice.

"You should have let him take me," Galene whispers. She lifts her chin, obeying Ceto's unspoken demands as she drags the sponge down her neck, between her breasts, around the arc of her ribs.

"Do you so long for punishment?" Ceto asks. Her thumb skims Galene's windpipe.

Galene begins to weep. She cries like a child, with abandon. Ceto holds her, riding out the storm of her grief.

"I thought there was something wrong with me, that I was incapable of love," Galene says.

Cradling her, Ceto presses her cheek to Galene's and slides her fingers around her neck. Galene stills in her arms.

"You and Naia showed me I was wrong."

Ceto tightens her fingers, dimpling the soft nape of her neck. Galene's trachea shifts between her thumbs.

"I know you've never loved me—not in the way I love you—but I forgive you for that." Galene closes her eyes.

The truth of her words shatters Ceto's resolve, and her hope of reclaiming sirenhood. She had withheld the deepest parts of herself from Galene; she had never trusted her with her love. She would mourn for Galene, but her grief would fade in a hundred years. A hundred more, and she would forget her entirely. The sacrifice would not be great enough.

Her hands slip from Galene's throat as she is consumed by the dawning horror of the only possible sacrifice she can make. It nearly brings her to her knees, but she will not bow to the pain.

She sways with the effort of holding herself upright, withstanding the sensation of knives plunging into her heels. Galene gathers a long, shaky breath, clutching her clothing to her chest.

"Go," Ceto says, and kisses her cheek. "Prepare for the show."

• • •

Naia's temples throb under the weight of her mother's crown. The horn shell rises from the center, nestled against star-like shells. The Pin Man's knife presses against her thigh.

In the bunker, she clings to her mother and Galene, imprinting the feel of their hands on her skin. She studies her aunts, memorizing their faces, packing away Maris's compassion when confronted with cruelty, Halia's persistent will to live, Galene's tenderness that showed her what love ought to be. She wishes she could take them all with her, but they chose this life long before she'd even thought to question it. They would never leave. And her mother will never forgive her. She'll make sure of that.

The sirens slide into the tube. Naia takes a deep breath, gathering herself, and plunges into the tank for her final performance. The sirens raise their arms to greet her.

In a castle fine as glass, sirens rule the sea. The older sisters are content with their reign, but the youngest longs for more. Her days are dark with silt, and unchanging. She is weary of the sea, with its sameness and its arctic cold. She is tired of half-light.

A shadow passes over the palace, and the youngest siren looks up as fireworks shatter the surface. Her sisters tell her no good can come of longing, but she pays them no heed. The waves try to face her down. Still, she pushes on, toward the line between earth and sky.

Lightning splits the sea and a prince plummets toward the black hole, trailing a ribbon of blood. The siren lets him drown.

With a crack of thunder that shudders the pearl chandelier, Ceto, as the sea witch, snakes from a billowing black cloud, reaching for the siren with branchlike fingers, her nails curved like eagle talons. Her eyes, augmented with contact lenses, are the opaque black of shark eyes.

What will the siren ask of the witch? The narration follows Naia's lead. *What is left to want?*

Naia unsheaths the Pin Man's knife. Anticipating its heft, she adjusts to its weightlessness beneath water. The blade gleams in the spotlight, drawing Ceto's gaze.

There will be no coming back from this. Tears blur her sight, and she is grateful to the sea for stealing them away. She shuts her eyes against an onslaught of despair. Everything she knows is here; everyone she loves. For the first time in a lifetime of performing, Naia freezes. The current nudges her. The narration waits on her cue. A palm slides over her knuckles and she knows by touch alone that it is her mother's. Within Ceto's hand, Naia's fingers loosen on the knife. She opens her eyes.

Ceto hangs before her, blank-eyed and glittering. The vision conjures a fleeting memory Naia had long ago forgotten. She was folded into a lobster cage behind the bar, serving punishment for a transgression she no longer remembers. Fingering the fabric of her tail, she'd watched her mother swim back and forth along the observation window scraping algae from the glass. She was mesmerized by Ceto's fluidity, the way the water eased the stringency from her muscles, her gleaming skin, the serenity of her expression. For the first time, Naia had recognized her mother as a separate being, rather than an extension of herself. She was awestruck.

The enchantment had worn off a long time ago. Now, when she looks at Ceto, she sees only a woman trapped in a spell of her own making. She had already severed herself from her mother in every way but one. Naia tightens her grip on the knife and shakes off Ceto's hand.

With a heartrending sense of finality, she plunges the knife into her tail where her thighs join. The fabric yields to the blade. The knifepoint scrapes her thigh, and nausea rises in her stomach but she shoves it down. She is an accomplished performer, and she has committed to this act. The knife slides between her legs as she slits her mother's tail from seam to fluke and peels away the sides to expose her pale flesh. Her skin glows in the dark water as the remnants of the tail drift, curling, toward the black hole.

Her mother can do nothing but watch as Naia stretches her legs to their full length, angling them to show off the pale undersides of her knees, opening her thighs to the audience. She plants her feet on the window and pushes away as if to crack the glass, shooting up through the tank toward the tube.

The sea witch will not let her go. She clasps the siren's ankle and gives her a rough tug, spinning her around in a sheet of bubbles. The crowd beyond the tank gasps as the witch drags her down and knots the siren's ankles with a rope of bull kelp, tethering her to the sea floor.

The siren raises her arms and fixes her dying gaze on the line between sea and sky. Her final breath leaves her lungs, and the current cradles her lifeless body. The witch buries her face at her feet.

The curtains close on the scene. The music fades, leaving the tank silent, but the pressure of the water is loud in Naia's ears. The kelp rope that binds her to the floor slides against her ankle bones. She unties the slippery knots with shaking fingers and casts a final glance at her mother's kingdom; the castle with its pearl-drop chandelier and waving anemones, and the dark side of the curtains now shut on the audience she'll never see again from this side of the glass.

Her mother and aunts drift above her, their hair blooming around their faces, their hands weaving the water to hold them still against the current. She wishes she could save them all, but she can only save herself. With a thrust of her tail, Naia dives into the mouth of the sea.

19

Naia descends through the hole against the current that tries to force her back. Darkness closes around her as she tunnels through the womb of Sirenland.

She will emerge from this rock, and she will don Claire's dress one last time. She will set out in the opposite direction from the boardwalk to follow the road that swerves around the cliff, past the chain restaurants, budget motels, and billboards for retirement communities.

The channel drives her into a turn so tight the rocks grate her scalp. Commanding herself to stay calm, she pushes on, anchoring her body against the rocks with her knees. She crawls through the unchanging dark.

She will sleep under the stars and beg for her breakfast. She'll learn to order in restaurants, and she'll eat scrambled eggs, bacon, toast, no butter, coffee, black; it will become her usual.

Scales glide over her skin. Her fingernails tear on the rocks and her lungs begin to ache. She pushes deep within herself, checking for the cache of air her body knows to hold in reserve. It is there, but her lungs suck greedily upon it.

She'll wear underwear and T-shirts, ball gowns and cowl-neck sweaters, tailored suits and bathing suits and jeans. She'll construct forts in fathomless woods and learn to ride a bicycle and fly an airplane.

She has never before come close to running out of air—but her lungs seize in need. Her chest contracts and water oozes up her nose, searing her throat.

She'll have lots of friends and kiss boys on long dark bus rides.

Her head pounds. The water lightens to a pale yellow, and a cloud of coin-like fish glimmers and parts as she flows through them. She pulls her feet beneath her and pushes up blindly, her body failing.

She'll buy a minivan and fill it with children greasy with sunscreen who'll fall asleep on their way home from adventures and she'll let her daughters cut their hair and she'll buy them books and talk to them until they tire of the sound of her voice.

Naia breaks the surface with a desperate gasp, her eyes streaming, and finds herself at the vent in the cliffside where they'd waited in vain for Nixie.

A yawning bass thrums through the water, an absence of sound, a hollowness her senses are incapable of interpreting. A few yards away, the Sailor's Ruin stands guard over the calm sea. With a final burst of strength, she drags her weary body to the rock and secures herself with bleeding fingers. She rests her cheek against its slick surface.

Slowly, she becomes aware of a pressure between her shoulder blades, kneading her strained muscles. She knows her mother's calloused touch—but she cannot imagine what to expect in this moment. Ceto may rail against her, may strike her or try to drag her back by the hair. She has never seen her mother cry. Naia gathers herself and turns.

Ceto rests her forehead against Naia's. Her eyes are still the sea witch's dizzying black.

"I'm sorry." Naia's voice emerges as a ragged croak. Her throat is raw with salt. "I knew you wouldn't let me go. But I've won my freedom."

Ceto closes her eyes, breathing slowly against Naia's cheek, and whispers a phrase she cannot begin to interpret:

"I, too, took a knife to my tail, and I have regretted it ever since." She cradles Naia's jaw in her palm. Her words, or the feeling behind them, are like the refrain of a familiar song Naia can't place, or a fragment of a dream that fades upon waking. Their meaning eludes her, swept away by the thrill of her mother's touch, finally tender. It is what Naia has always wanted, and far too late.

"I will not beg you to stay, but I entreat you to grant me one request," Ceto says. "A final swim before we part."

She extends her hand to Naia, letting fall a scrap of her black tail. It flows through her fingers and drifts into the waves like seaweed. Naia accepts her mother's hand.

"I promise I'll come back," she says as her mother draws her out to sea.

Ceto replies, "Don't make promises you cannot keep."

Naia allows her mother to lead her through the waves as if she were no more than a child. Ceto's tail streams behind her. Her fingernails cut into Naia's palm.

She had not made an empty promise; she will return to Sirenland, but as a tourist like the rest. She will stay at one of the grand hotels on the opposite side of the boardwalk and walk her children across the beach to visit their grandmother and great-aunts. Her children will enjoy Sirenland. She, too, had loved it once.

As her mother tows her against the current toward the barrier, the bass of distant music intensifies, vibrating down Naia's spine. It strengthens into a command that pounds into her body as if it were the ocean itself.

Her mother stops without warning, and Naia slams into the net barrier like a caught fish. She strains against the fibers as her mother leads her down to the colder water where she can just make out two figures pushing through the gloom beyond the net. A vision flashes behind her eyes of Claire floating below the surface with her hair clouded around her, a rope sawing into her bones.

As the figures flow closer, the bass fills her ears, pulsing into her head like a heartbeat as they press against the net. *Her bones are coral made, a sea-change into something rich and strange.* The lines of song return to her, coalescing *ding-dong—ding-dong—*

They appear to be Naia's age, with the same chin, same strong shoulders, same distinctive brow. Their heavy breasts are bare and their long fingers are tipped with dagger-like nails. Despite their inhumanity, they resemble Ceto; more terrifyingly still, they look like Naia.

Naia gasps, breathing in the sea, and rises choking and blind to the surface. Salt sears her throat. The surface is calm, with no hint of what lies below. Naia clings to the net. The Ferris wheel turns with tinny music on the pier. The moon glows over the sea that had served as her backdrop every day of her life. It all seems so ordinary.

Ceto rises to the surface beside Naia. Her daughter recoils as the sirens surge up beyond the net, but Ceto holds her fast.

"Sister, she is a pretty one," the sirens croon, stroking their own cheeks with their blackened fingernails.

Ceto turns to Naia as if they were alone.

"It is time you know who you are," she says. "Your origins begin and end with me."

Naia grips her hand as if to quiet her, to press the words back into her skin.

"I denied you your immortality," Ceto says. "Sirenland is the only birthright I could give you."

Ceto turns to her sisters. "But she does not appreciate it. She has been moving away from me since the minute she was born."

"Foolish girl." The sirens shake their heads in a show of contempt. There is blood in their hair.

They fix their eyes on Naia's. Her body goes limp, and she drifts toward the net.

"Sister, what is your choice?" they hiss, reaching for Naia.

Ceto slides Naia's knife from the waist of her tail. Her sisters grip Naia through the net, holding her fast with greedy smiles.

Ceto steels herself. Living with her daughter's desertion would be far more painful than the momentary agony of losing Naia followed by eternal oblivion. She'd given her everything; gifted her a world where she could invent herself. In renouncing Sirenland, her daughter has rejected everything they are. But she is still a child, and Ceto is still her mother. She knows what her daughter needs. She *made* Naia, after all.

"I choose for my daughter to understand what I have sacrificed for her to live," Ceto says, and plunges the knife into her own breast.

20

A keening, panicked sound that Naia barely recognizes as human wrenches from her throat as her mother's body arches against the knife. The sirens release her from their spell with a wordless shriek, their talons raking her skin as she shoves them away. Naia casts her arms around her mother. They sink together.

Pain tears through her as if her all her bones are cracking at once. The anguish of it buckles her. Ceto's weight drags her down and the sea blooms red around them.

Fire slices across her waist, below her navel, doubling her in half, imploding her. Pressure grinds into her center. Rendered to base instinct, she loses her grip on her mother and wraps her arms around her stomach, where the pain strains against her ribs and pelvis, filling her with stormy waves. She is cleaved from the inside.

Her legs fuse and lengthen, gathering glittering black scales. Pain sears the flesh behind her ears and she reaches up to find slits sundering her neck. Her teeth pull into points, tearing at their roots.

The sirens rip through the barrier and grasp her wrists. As they draw her through the tattered remains of the net, she strains toward Ceto even as the instinct to rejoin her mother recedes from her. Hunger takes hold. She forgets what she was reaching for.

• • •

Ceto's body pulls apart and dissolves, returning to the sea that made her. She is connected to something again. The waves carry her in ever-widening rings to reverberate off distant shores. She rides the currents through the centuries, waiting for fleeting impressions of Naia.

She cannot remember the sensation of her daughter straining against her ribs from the inside. She cannot remember the weight of Naia's body against her chest, or the love that had turned her inside out with fear. She cannot remember the beat of her daughter's heart against her cheek, but the echo of it resounds in her cells. In this way, she keeps Naia with her, always.

ACKNOWLEDGMENTS

For FB, who noted that the men in this book are inconsequential. I assure you, that's no reflection of your consequence. You are the best one. The only one for me.

For Mom and Dad for everything. Most of all, for your partnership in raising Imogen. We cannot express how much we love you and how grateful we are for the Dedes. I don't know what we would do without you.

For Immy. I'd build a kingdom for you, but you will build your own.

For Brenna Enos, my original siren sister. I am constantly in awe of your drive, your talent, your capacity for love. I may be taller, but I look up to you.

For fearless, ferocious, beautiful Sophia Macris, who inspires me and everyone around her to live boldly.

For Kate Gale and Red Hen Press team, who champion strange books and stranger writers, who guide us with enthusiasm and great care. I couldn't be prouder for my books to have found a home with you. For Serene Hakim, for believing in Ceto—and me—from the beginning, and for your thoughtful and invaluable editorial insight. For Ann Hood, who chose *Animal Wife* and kick-started my career. I will always be grateful.

For Amber Sparks—thank you for your support, your honest and relatable posts that keep me going when motherhood gets hard, and for your strange, always-inspiring, women-centered work.

For Elma Burnham and Captain Dave Marciano, who shared their expertise about the fishing trade, and for Dr. Robert Knight of the

Florida Springs Institute, who patiently explained the ins and outs of Florida's aquifer system.

For the Garret on the Green Residency, Bread Loaf Writers' Conference, and Martha's Vineyard Institute of Creative Writing, who offered me the gift of time, space, and support to write this book. For all the coffee shops that fueled me with bottomless coffee; especially True Grounds in Somerville, MA.

For my daughter's loving daycare providers Lisa Belen, Justine Salamone, Sarah Blasi, and Lisa Impemba-Costa, and the entire Little Busy Bodies family.

For the guests on my podcast *Writer Mother Monster* who share their stories of monstrous motherhood and inspire me—and our listeners—with their passion, ambition, and fierce love for their children. writermothermonster.com

For Florida's roadside marvel Weeki Wachee Springs State Park, where women have been performing as mermaids since 1947, and for Rita King and her fellow Legendary Sirens who taught me to dance in a tail. For my sister sirens-in-training, Stephanie Ross, Sally Wallin, and Heidi Hammond.

And for Hans Christian Andersen.

The Weeki Wachee Spring water originates from limestones of the Floridian aquifer system, one of the world's most productive aquifers. It spans Florida and parts of neighboring states and feeds fresh water into rivers, lakes, and springs throughout the region. Due to overextraction, pollution, climate change, and other factors, the aquifers are at risk. Learn more about Weeki Wachee and help save Florida's springs by visiting floridastateparks.org.

BIOGRAPHICAL NOTE

Lara Ehrlich is the author of the short story collection *Animal Wife*, which won the Red Hen Press Fiction Award judged by Ann Hood. Her work explores themes of transformation, performance, motherhood, and feminist mythmaking, and has appeared in numerous literary journals and anthologies. Lara is the host of *Writer Mother Monster*, a conversation series devoted to dismantling the myth of "having it all," and the founder and director of Thought Fox Writers Den, a creative writing center offering workshops, coaching, and community for writers of all levels. She lives in Connecticut with her family.
www.LaraEhrlich.com

www.ingramcontent.com/pod-product-compliance
Lightning Source LLC
Jackson TN
JSHW021914260725
88266JS00002B/4